THE COSMIC CRUSADERS

Borgo Press Books by JOHN RUSSELL FEARN

1,000-Year Voyage: A Science Fiction Novel * *Anjani the Mighty: A Lost Race Novel* (Anjani #2) * *Black Maria, M.A.: A Classic Crime Novel* (Black Maria #1) * *A Case for Brutus Lloyd* * *The Crimson Rambler: A Crime Novel* * *Death in Silhouette* (Black Maria #5) * *Don't Touch Me: A Crime Novel* * *Dynasty of the Small: Classic Science Fiction Stories* * *The Empty Coffins: A Mystery of Horror* * *The Fourth Door: A Mystery Novel* * *From Afar: A Science Fiction Mystery* * *Fugitive of Time: A Classic Science Fiction Novel* * *The G-Bomb: A Science Fiction Novel* * *The Genial Dinosaur* (Herbert the Dinosaur #2) * *The Gold of Akada: A Jungle Adventure Novel* (Anjani #1) * *Here and Now: A Science Fiction Novel* * *Into the Unknown: A Science Fiction Tale* * *Last Conflict: Classic Science Fiction Stories* * *Legacy from Sirius: A Classic Science Fiction Novel* * *The Man from Hell: Classic Science Fiction Stories* * *The Man Who Was Not: A Crime Novel* * *Manton's World: A Classic Science Fiction Novel* * *Moon Magic: A Novel of Romance* (as Elizabeth Rutland) * *The Murdered Schoolgirl: A Classic Crime Novel* (Black Maria #2) * *One Remained Seated: A Classic Crime Novel* (Black Maria #3) * *One Way Out: A Crime Novel* (with Philip Harbottle) * *Pattern of Murder: A Classic Crime Novel* * *Reflected Glory: A Dr. Castle Classic Crime Novel* * *Robbery Without Violence: Two Science Fiction Crime Stories* * *Rule of the Brains: Classic Science Fiction Stories* * *Shattering Glass: A Crime Novel* * *The Silvered Cage: A Scientific Murder Mystery* * *Slaves of Ijax: A Science Fiction Novel* * *Something from Mercury: Classic Science Fiction Stories* * *The Space Warp: A Science Fiction Novel* * *A Thing of the Past* (Herbert the Dinosaur #1) * *Thy Arm Alone: A Classic Crime Novel* (Black Maria #4) * *The Time Trap: A Science Fiction Novel* * *Vision Sinister: A Scientific Detective Thriller* * *Voice of the Conqueror: A Classic Science Fiction Novel* * *What Happened to Hammond? A Scientific Mystery* * *Within That Room!: A Classic Crime Novel* * *World Without Chance*

THE GOLDEN AMAZON SAGA

1. *World Beneath Ice* * 2. *Lord of Atlantis* * 3. *Triangle of Power* * 4. *The Amethyst City* * 5. *Daughter of the Amazon* * 6. *Quorne Returns* * 7. *The Central Intelligence* * 8. *The Cosmic Crusaders* * 9. *Parasite Planet* * 10. *World Out of Step* * 11. *The Shadow People* * 12. *Kingpin Planet* * 13. *World in Reverse* * 14. *Dwellers in Darkness* * 15. *World in Duplicate* * 16. *Lords of Creation* * 17. *Duel with Colossus* * 18. *Standstill Planet* * 19. *Ghost World* * 20. *Earth Divided* * 21. *Chameleon Planet* (with Philip Harbottle)

THE COSMIC CRUSADERS

THE GOLDEN AMAZON SAGA, BOOK EIGHT

JOHN RUSSELL FEARN

Edited by Philip Harbottle

THE BORGO PRESS

MMXIII

THE COSMIC CRUSADERS

FIRST BORGO PRESS EDITION

Published by Wildside Press LLC

www.wildsidebooks.com

DEDICATION

To the memory of Ron Turner

CONTENTS

THE GOLDEN AMAZON, by Philip Harbottle 9

CHAPTER ONE: Viona's Idea 16

CHAPTER TWO: Farewell to Earth 25

CHAPTER THREE: Planetfall 35

CHAPTER FOUR: Hypnosis 43

CHAPTER FIVE: Woman of Axilon 51

CHAPTER SIX: The Devil's Workshop 58

CHAPTER SEVEN: Revolution 70

CHAPTER EIGHT: The Capture of Viona 81

CHAPTER NINE: The Radium Ocean 91

CHAPTER TEN: Banishment 102

CHAPTER ELEVEN: Marooned on Nur 110

CHAPTER TWELVE: Vengeance of the Amazon 118

CHAPTER THIRTEEN: The Saving of Viona . . 125

CHAPTER FOURTEEN: In Mental Chains . . . 132

CHAPTER FIFTEEN: World of the Mizanu . . . 140

CHAPTER SIXTEEN: Viona's Plan 147

CHAPTER SEVENTEEN: The Asteroid 154

CHAPTER EIGHTEEN: Viona in Thrall 162

CHAPTER NINETEEN: Viona Fights Back. . . 171

CHAPTER TWENTY: Cosmic Collision 179

ABOUT THE AUTHOR 186

THE GOLDEN AMAZON
by Philip Harbottle

In 1943 British writer John Russell Fearn decided to quit writing for the American pulp science fiction magazines, and to concentrate instead on books for the English market. Within a very few years he became established as a leading novelist in several genres, not only science fiction, but also mystery and detective fiction, and westerns.

His first new SF novel, *The Golden Amazon*, was published by World's Work in April 1944. In this story, a little girl of three years of age is made the subject of an idealistic scientist's illegal glandular experiments. The scientist's dream is to end world wars by creating a woman devoid of the usual lusts and frailties of mankind, who upon reaching maturity would institute a benign scientific rule. But the apparently successful experiment has a flaw: it instills into the girl a hatred for all men, and a ruthless cruelty. Her supernatural scientific gifts enable her to master atomic power, and practically leads her to destroy the world. She breaks the will and strength of men, and elevates women to positions of wealth and power. She also discovers human synthesis, and by this means she is able to escape retribution when she is eventually overthrown. She is seen to collapse and die, a victim of consuming ketabolism, echoing the memorable finale of Rider Haggard's *She*. In actuality, it was only her synthetic image, and this paved the way for the *Golden Amazon Returns*, and further sequels

Fearn sold reprint rights in the first novel to the prestigious Canadian magazine, the Toronto *Star Weekly*. The magazine carried a special Comics Supplement, the centre section of which was a 'complete novel', published in newspaper format. Aimed at a general readership, the novels were written by the top popular novelists of the day, including John Dickson Carr, Ellery Queen, and P. G. Wodehouse. They sold hundreds of thousands of copies, and the novels were syndicated to several American newspapers in the Maine and New York areas. The Amazon novels enjoyed extraordinary popularity (especially with Canadian housewives), and ran for the next sixteen years following the appearance of the first novel in the March 3, 1945 issue, ending with Fearn's sudden death in September 1960, aged only fifty-two. His final two Amazon novels appeared posthumously.

During Fearn's lifetime, only the first six novels were published in British hardcover editions from the World's Work in England, after appearing in the *Star Weekly*. This was because the publishers discontinued their entire fiction line in 1954. However, the Amazon novels continued to appear in the *Star Weekly*, eventually notching up twenty-four titles.

Fearn had resold paperback rights to the Canadian publisher Harlequin Books, but after publishing only the first three titles, they stopped publishing SF and other genre fiction to concentrate on their famous Romances line.

Meanwhile, as early as 1949, Fearn had realized that the Amazon series had the potential to run indefinitely. This presented him with a problem, however. The 'origin story' of the Golden Amazon was conceived and actually set during the Second World War. Subsequent novels were written during the war and the immediate postwar period, and projected their stories only a few decades into the future.

He very astutely realized that to keep ahead of reality, he needed to move the Amazon *further* into the future—first into the outer solar system, and thence to the stars. So with the seventh novel, he introduced a new main character, Abna of Atlantis—someone as equally intelligent, and even stronger than herself. These dynamics provided him with an *interstellar* canvas, thus ensuring that the series would remain ahead of reality.

Fearn's strategy was a great success, and the Amazon novels retained their popularity, ending only with his tragically early death in 1960. By then he had written a further twenty Amazon novels, and made prelimi-nary notes for his next (which would later be written by Fearn's biographer, Philip Harbottle).

Long after Fearn's death, his entire Amazon series

would eventually see print from the pioneering US small press Gryphon Books in limited paperback editions, and later by the Canadian Battered Silicon Dispatch Box small press in their hardcover Omnibus series.

This new Borgo Press paperback series will be the first trade edition of all twenty-one of these later novels by Fearn, beginning with the seventh novel in the original series. First published in 1949 as *Conquest of the Amazon*, I have edited it slightly as *World Beneath Ice* (The Golden Amazon Saga, Book One) so that it can be read and enjoyed by new readers who may be totally unfamiliar with what had gone before. Subsequent novels have also been slightly edited for modern readers.

The publishers hope that this new series may create many more "fans of the Amazon." Meanwhile, any reader interested in seeking out the earlier six Golden Amazon novels will find that they are readily available on the internet, and in numerous earlier paperback and hardcover editions.

* * * * * * * * *

To date, readers can enjoy the following new Borgo Press editions:

Book One: *World Beneath Ice*

In destroying the threat of an alien invasion, the Golden Amazon had inadvertently caused a decline in the sun's heat, encasing Earth in an ice sheet that threatens to eliminate humanity. The Amazon encounters Abna, a descendant of Atlantis, stronger and even more scientifically advanced than she, and the ruler of an Atlantean colony still surviving in a protected environment on Jupiter. She refuses his offer of marriage, but agrees to form an alliance in order to restore the sun and save the Earth. One thing that Abna has not told the Amazon is that all the females of his race have been wiped out by a bacilli infection....

Book Two: *Lord of Atlantis*

A gigantic ridge of land rises from the Atlantic floor, causing massive tidal waves on either side of the ocean. Even stranger, both England and America are then assailed by an invasion of prehistoric monsters! A gigantic domed city rests on the newly risen plateau, whilst out in space an alien spacecraft orbits the Earth. Such are the mysteries and challenges facing the Golden Amazon, self-appointed governess of Earth, as she struggles to unravel the maze of mystery that was the deadly legacy of Atlantis!

Book Three: *Triangle of Power*

The marriage of Violet Ray Brant—better known as The Golden Amazon—and Abna of Atlantis should have ushered in an era of peace and scientific prosperity to the people of Earth. But an unexpected turn of events finds Abna betrayed and marooned on a satellite of Jupiter, and the Amazon flung far beyond the Solar System. With Earth's two protectors removed, the planet is now at the mercy of another Atlantean, the master scientist Sefner Quorne....

Book Four: *The Amethyst City*

The metaphysical union of the Amazon and Abna results in the mental creation of a fully mature daughter— Viona. Quorne, still struggling for domination, forces Viona into a marriage ceremony, and impregnates her. But with the intervention of Tarnec Brodix, a super-mind from an external universe, Quorne and Viona are separately flung into an ultra-dimensional limbo. Abna chooses to follow after his daughter, leaving the Amazon to brood over the disaster, alone in the Amethyst City of Saturn.

Book Five: *Daughter of the Amazon*

A miscalculation by the super-mathematician Tarnec Brodix destroys his universe, and the fault spreads into the Earth universe in the form of a Dark Tide of Absolute Nothingness. Unable to save himself, Brodix transfers his knowledge into the one mind powerful enough to receive it: that if Sefian, the son who has been born to Viona and Quorne. Sefian rapidly evolves, and, no longer human, after saving the Earth universe, vanishes into the greater universe, to seek new challenges. Then the Amazon is confronted with a further puzzle—a large section of the planet Neptune is discovered to be an exact duplicate of the Earth!

Book Six: *Quorne Returns*

The bacterial intelligences of Neptune plan to conquer Earth by replacing humans in key positions with alien duplicates. The Neptunians are themselves subjugated by the sinister Atlantean scientist, Sefner Quorne. Alerted to the threat, the Golden Amazon hits back by creating the ultimate doomsday weapon—only to precipitate a reprisal from the denizens of another universe....

Book Seven: *The Central Intelligence*

The Golden Amazon's arch-enemy, Sefner Quorne, discovers that all mental gifts, such as memory and creativity, are something that is broadcast throughout the universe by a Central Intelligence—and then interpreted according to the quality of the individual brain of the recipient. At the surprising suggestion of his wife, Viona, the Amazon's daughter, Quorne travels with her to the very center of the universe, in order to wrest the secrets of mentality from the very source itself!

CHAPTER ONE
VIONA'S IDEA

With the passing of Sefner Quorne, master scientist of Jupiter, from the scheme of things, his destruction at the will of the Central Intelligence being absolute, there began for the three greatest scientists on Earth a new era of activity.

"Why don't we do as I suggested long ago and form the Cosmic Crusaders?"

It was Viona who spoke—Viona of the copper-gold hair and sapphire blue eyes. Viona, daughter of the fantastic Golden Amazon and Abna of Jupiter. Viona—young, vastly strong, impetuously brilliant, already the mistress of a dozen complicated sciences and the widow of Sefner Quorne. But to her the memory of him was bitter. She had never really been his wife: he had simply used her—and now he would use her no more.

"The Cosmic Crusaders, eh?" It was Abna who spoke this time, the metaphysical wizard of Jupiter, seven feet of overpowering blond manhood, and the only male in all the Solar System who had ever beaten the Golden Amazon at her own game. In most things he was her equal, and in a few isolated instances her master, though she had never admitted it and never would.

"At least," the Golden Amazon herself said, "it would be a change from monotony, Abna. Earth has little need of our assistance and guardianship these days."

For a moment there was silence in the solarium at the summit of the great building where the Amazon had her London headquarters. Below, there stretched the enormity of citadels that was the metropolis. Overhead there came and went the fleets of soundless aircraft. Occasionally a rocket-powered spaceship took off in a soul-tearing scream, which faded as the vessel climbed beyond the limits of the atmosphere. Here was the world of a future time—placid, organized, and prosperous.

"You once said," Abna remarked, "that we should start a kind of super 'help your neighbor' campaign and call ourselves the Cosmic Crusaders. A kind of helping hand to those planetary inhabitants who haven't our knowledge and resources."

"Right!" Viona confirmed. "Anything wrong with the suggestion?"

"Nothing at all; very laudable. The only point is, my dear, I can't think of any planetary populations which need helping. From here to Pluto they are all under our aegis and our benefits are theirs. Whom are we supposed to help?"

"That is what has been baffling me, too," the Amazon

commented, turning her beautiful face toward the two at the further end of the sunny roof-top solarium.

Viona sat up and smote her head in disgust. "I live with the greatest scientific geniuses in the System and they can't even see what I'm driving at! You're slipping, the pair of you! I'm not talking about our immediate Solar System, about which we know all there is to know: I'm thinking of the worlds beyond! Far out in space where telescopic power cannot reach. Worlds nearer to the Milky Way than to us. The galaxial deeps, so far removed from here that our System would not be apparent to them any more than theirs is to us."

The Amazon said: "We've been into the Outer Deeps before, Viona, and have never seen a trace of a planetary system like our own—unless you include odd dead planets here and there, little better than hulks."

"Until we get out into the Deeps ourselves, mother, we can't state anything for certain. I'm thinking, initially, of possible Systems that may exist in the region of Alpha Centauri. Alpha being the nearest star to us—together with Proxima, which makes for Alpha being a double-sun—there's no reason why a System should not exist around him as our System exists around our own sun."

"Quite possible," Abna agreed, flexing his mighty arms.

"Very well then—" Viona spread her hands. "What are we waiting for?"

Abna grinned. "We are waiting, Viona, for suggestions as to how we reach the potential worlds around

Alpha Centauri. Or have you overlooked that Alpha is twenty thousand billion miles away? A matter just over four years to reach him, even moving at the speed of light."

"Of course I haven't overlooked it! I haven't overlooked, either, that there have been occasions in the past when we've often exceeded the speed of light by many times! Have you forgotten that the *Ultra*'s controls and power plant have been converted for four-dimensional travel? I employed them when I took the plunge with Quorne to the center of the universe in our encounter with the Central Intelligence. By warping the *Ultra* into the fourth dimension, we were able to travel at near-infinite velocity relative to the normal three-dimensional universe. Light is no more the governing speed factor of the *Ultra* than the speed of sound is the limit for aircraft...."

"All right!" Abna protested. "Your mother and I are not exactly novices when it comes to scientific facts. Certainly the speed of light can be exceeded in the *Ultra*, but can we stand it for the long period necessary to make the vast hops between stars?"

"Why not?" Viona gave a shrug. "If we were normal people, I'd say we'd flatten out and die. But we're super-humanly strong, accustomed to space travel—and we can simply sleep part of the journey, don't forget. Anyway, even if it did kill us eventually, it'd be better than rusting to death on Earth here, wouldn't it?"

The Amazon said: "The surprising thing is the child's right."

"I'm no child!"

"To us, I mean." The Amazon gave a faint smile and then continued: "In the *Ultra* we could exceed the speed of light by using the automatic control to side-slip from the normal space-time continuum into the fourth dimension once the course to Alpha was set. That would have the effect of foreshortening space, and then we'd emerge back into normal space once the gulf had been traversed. As Viona remarked, there may be worlds out there in the Greater Deeps that we could benefit. Backward populations, to whom science as yet means nothing. We might, in due time, bring true that dream I once had—long before I met you, Abna. Long before Viona was—created."

"What dream, mother?" Viona was bright-eyed with eagerness as the Amazon slipped a supple arm around her young shoulders.

"It was a dream of unifying the whole Universe—the whole mighty macrocosmic molecule which Einstein once called finite and yet unbounded. In those days I believed in power for power's sake; I believed the populations of endless worlds would have to bow down before my scientific skill. Since then I have learned a great deal. Ruthlessness is not always the answer, and perhaps I have been mellowed by the passing years."

"Mellowed maybe," Viona admitted, "but you're still the most brilliant woman this planet has ever known. Don't go back on your fabulous reputation by behaving like an ordinary person."

The Amazon smiled whimsically, dropping her arm

from about Viona's shoulders.

"I shall never do that, provided— always provided— that I can find something upon which to exercise my talents. Your idea of a flight to Alpha Centauri is like the old days—the freedom of space, the call of adventure, the magnificent tension of never knowing what is to happen next. Maybe we might make a beginning in trying to unify the Universe. We might even start to obliterate all those cruel, selfish elements that make everlasting peace among thinking beings impossible. Yes, Viona, I'm all for the flight to Outer Space. What about you, Abna?"

"Anything goes. Certainly there is little we can do on Earth except mope around and make experiments."

So it was decided, and preparations immediately went forward for the greatest journey ever yet contemplated by these three super-scientists who ruled the System.

The one individual to whom most information was vouchsafed was Chris Wilson, wealthy controller of the System's Space Lines. He seemed puzzled when, the day before departure, the Amazon outlined everything to him.

"Frankly, Vi," he said, using as ever the Amazon's Christian name, "it does not make sense to me. You and Abna—and maybe even Viona by now—have the mastery of mind over matter so complete that you can project yourselves anywhere at any time by using sufficient concentration. Since there are no barriers to thought, why go to all the trouble of a space journey in the *Ultra* when you can mentally project yourselves to your destination?"

"Good old Chris!" The Amazon gave a sigh. "Always have your two feet planted firmly on Earth, don't you? The reason why the journey must be a normal physical one is because we don't yet know where our destination is to be."

"You said Alpha Centauri. What more is needed?"

"A good deal more! We have to be certain that there is a planetary system around Alpha. There's no guarantee of one. If we used mental projection we'd reassemble in space itself without a world to tread. True, mental power could again save us from destruction, but it would be a profound waste of intellectual energy.... No, this has to be done in the normal way. And anyhow, there is the interest of the voyage! Think of it—many times faster than light and a distance of twenty thousand billion miles! What might we not see on a trip like that?"

Chris Wilson winced. "Probably fascinates you, Vi, but I'm an aging codger who prefers the fireside and daily routine. Incidentally, I assume no communication with you will be possible?"

"Not after we've left the solar system—which will be with extreme rapidity—and then warped into the fourth dimension. Everything else has been attended to, and the high-level executives of the government know they have to rely henceforth on their own resources."

The Amazon rose to her feet, as erect as a golden statue. She held out her slim hand—that hand that could, under necessity, crush flash and blood to pulp.

"Goodbye, Chris," she said simply, her profound eyes upon him.

He had risen too and, puzzled, he shook hands and then regarded her.

"Goodbye? That sounds like the end of the road. Surely it isn't that?"

"It may be. Once we are launched way beyond the nearest star, we shall not come back to Earth without very good reason. Earth no longer has need of us. Our future lies amongst the stars, trying to build up those backward scientific races that need aid. Everything we do shall be in the name of this home world of ours, of course, but.... Well, the journeying may take many years. Even centuries. You are a natural human being, Chris, and for that reason your life span is short compared to Abna's, Viona's, and mine. So it *is* goodbye, you see."

Chris shook his white-haired head vehemently. "I'll never believe that, Vi. You'll be back before I die, with some new wonder to relate."

The Amazon only shrugged and walked to the door. Reaching it, she turned and smiled at the bemused Chris. "I haven't time to say goodbye to your family, Chris. But I've left a video message in my office for Ethel and the others. Give her my regards...." In another moment she had left the colossal administrative Space Edifice, and was on her way in her private atomic helicopter to the great hangar where reposed her space machine, the *Ultra*. The hangar lay outside the city itself, an enormous building housing the most powerful space machine ever known. Into its design had gone the combined genius of three scientific intellectuals, and within it was every conceivable necessity. It was a flying city in itself.

CHAPTER TWO
FAREWELL TO EARTH

Arriving at the hangar, the Amazon found both Abna and Viona hard at work on final preparations for departure. Whilst Abna was checking the atomic power plant and fourth-dimensional switchboard, Viona was attending to the hundred and one details concerning provisions, clothing, air supply, weapon ammunition, and so forth.

"Everything fixed?" Viona asked, as her mother entered the big control room.

"Yes, everything—and the goodbyes have been said. Your father busy on the power unit?"

"Uh-huh."

"Then I'd better do my part of the work and get the course mapped out."

The Amazon went to work, walking into the navigation chamber adjacent to the control room. Here there loomed all the scientific paraphernalia and computers necessary to make dead certain of any predicted path through space. Here were mathematical machines of incredible accuracy, designed to weigh up every possible contingency in the complicated equational formula of traveling between dimensions.

For an hour the Amazon brooded over the calculations she was working out, checking the results with the computers. When at last she had come to the end of her maze of figuring she seemed satisfied. The sound of footsteps on the metal floor caused her to turn.

The gigantic figure of Abna entered, his handsome face smudged with grease from his activities.

"Everything in order," he announced. "Near as I can estimate we'll need twenty copper disintegrative blocks for this trip, which is as much as we can carry without them interacting with each other. After that we'll have to look elsewhere for fresh supplies. The twenty blocks allow enough and to spare to make the trip to Alpha Centauri and wherever we go next."

The Amazon figured quickly and then looked surprised. "But twenty blocks is a tremendous number, Abna! In free space, once we've achieved our required velocity, we'll move at a constant speed without the power plant."

"I'm aware of it, but don't overlook that the period of acceleration will be enormously draining of power, due to our having to quickly build up velocity to that approaching light. Then will come the leap into four-dimensional space. That will be another tremendous drain on the power supply. Then again, we do not know that space approaching Alpha Centauri will be absolutely clear. There may be the colossal hulks of burned-out suns to fight against, their gravities infinitely greater than anything we have ever encountered before. There are dozens of unknown factors, hence the precautions."

The Amazon nodded. "Better to be safe than sorry," she agreed. "As to future copper supplies, we ought to be able to find copper-bearing Systems somewhere with which to replenish. I imagine that copper is about one of the most prolific elements throughout the Universe."

Abna crossed to the charting console and studied the course. In a matter of minutes his agile brain had linked the equations in place and he patted the Amazon's softly molded arm.

"Good girl! We'll make a space pilot of you yet!"

Her violet eyes smoldered. "For your information, Abna of Jupiter, let me tell you—"

"You needn't," Abna grinned. "You built the *Ultra* and have flown it by accident into the deeps! Yes, I know—but that was an enforced journey and more or less of an accident. This, let us hope, will be interesting even if the initial buildup in acceleration is crushing."

He said no more. Leaving the navigation chamber, he set himself the task of checking over the multi-switchboards, a job which took him the rest of the day. Indeed, with only short intervals between, the three worked ceaselessly on their preparations right up to the time of departure, which was ten p.m. the following evening. Then, in the mellow summer dusk, they arrived at the hangar, ready attired in their space clothes—light tunics for Abna and Viona, and skin-fitting black tights for the Amazon, relieved by the single solid gold belt about her slender waist.

"I have the feeling," the Amazon remarked, as they all three stood in the big airlock and watched the hangar around them automatically fold itself away into sections, "that we're looking our last on Earth for a very, very long time to come."

"A most cheerful note on which to depart," Abna commented.

"True, nevertheless. We'll go forward, Abna, once we've reached Alpha—not backward."

There was silence for a moment. The only sound on the still summer evening air came from the city itself—a deep, resonant throb of industry. Here and there the lights were automatically coming up. Away to the east an Earth-Mars space liner was just coming in, its portholes glowing warmly.

"All right." Abna said at last, his voice quiet, "let's be on our way."

The Amazon and Viona went ahead of him into the control room. Abna pulled over the switch that sealed the airlock, then he gave a final glance over the instruments.

"We know exactly what we're doing?" he asked.

"Certainly," the Amazon assented. "Everything is to be automatic until the first copper block has spent itself. By that time we ought to be beyond the orbit of Pluto, and really well launched on our journey. Then the automatic controls will switch the ship into the fourth dimension—during which time we might as well relax in sleep, since there'll be nothing to see—then we will awaken when we drop back into normal space."

"Correct," Abna agreed. "Let's get settled."

Without any fuss they went into a compartment in the center of the vessel where they settled themselves on powerfully sprung beds, strapping themselves down so that, as acceleration finally ceased, they would not float away from their moorings.

Beside each bed was a bank of controls, as compactly contained as though on a typewriter keyboard. By this means they could each do their respective parts in controlling the mighty vessel, the slave switchboards being connected to the masters in the control room.

Abna, lying calmly with his forearms in the movable rests, held his fingertips above the buttons and looked at the chronometer in the ceiling.

"Fifteen seconds to go," he said, and moved the button which started up the power plant. Immediately a dull whining pervaded the sealed-in silence.

"Six," Abna said presently. "Five—four—three—two—one—"

It was the Amazon's hand that moved next, closing the switch that transferred the atomic power to the recoil jets. Instantly the vast space machine began to rise—traveling diagonally as far as the trio was concerned—since the internal chambers were all built on universal mountings. Externally, the *Ultra* was almost at the vertical, its rear tubes blazing an inconceivable holocaust of expanding fire and poisonous gases.

Faster and faster still the machine cleaved the dusk of the evening, hurtling upwards into the unclouded sky, leaving Earth as a titanic, lighted patchwork below. The three on the pressure beds absorbed the awful sensation calmly, accustomed to it from their many space journeys in the past. And in any case, nothing like the maximum velocity had yet been achieved.

Switches clicked under Viona's slim fingers. Instantly the *Ultra* gave a mighty surge. Here within the insulated walls there was no sound, but outside the awful roar of the *Ultra*'s departure into space was heard for over two hundred miles, a cleaving channel of scattering fire defining the track into the upper heavens.

Faster and yet faster, each movement of a relay piling speed upon speed, velocity upon velocity. Even when the full depth of the Earth's atmospheric belt had been penetrated—at which point acceleration was usually slackened off—the power was still increased. Motionless, beginning now to feel the terrible dragging weight of acceleration upon them, the three moved their buttons in the correct sequences, watching meanwhile the fantastic gyrations of the velocity readings as miles per second flashed into hundreds, thousands, and tens of thousands of miles per second. They were traveling now at a prodigious velocity, and with every moment it was still increasing.

They were beyond the orbit of the Moon and flashing onward toward the orbit of Mars. Still the speed increased. Switches clicked. Hearts labored. Breathing became a vast effort, herculean though the three were in strength.... The metal walls around them were spinning in a blaze of lights that slowly faded as they deliberately let themselves slip into unconsciousness.

With nothing to guide it in the way of a human hand, the *Ultra* thereafter flashed onwards with awful velocity, the automatic controls functioning perfectly under the guidance of computers. The three on their sprung beds remained motionless, their forearms still clamped to the rests above the slave stitches, a precaution so that they might, upon return to consciousness, be able to handle the switches if at all possible. Without the rests, dragging weight could have made their arms useless and their hands mere dead lumps of clay.

Beyond Mars' orbit, still with the velocity mounting. Then onwards past the asteroids, avoiding all danger by sweeping with prodigious speed far above the ecliptic plane of that deadly 'minefield' of floating bodies, and so out to the territory occupied by gigantic Jupiter. Here the automatic repulsion equipment came into action and kept the hurtling vessel clear of the deadly drag of the monster's gravity.

Within a matter of minutes, so unbelievable was the speed which had now been attained, Jupiter was receding into the gulf arid. Superb Saturn was ahead. Non-stop, onwards and outwards, commencing now to approximate the incredible speed of light itself— 186,000 miles a second.

The orbits of the outer worlds were passed. Saturn— Uranus—Neptune—Pluto—. The three remained unconscious, pressed down into a state approximating that of suspended animation, scarcely breathing, their hearts laboring under the load of acceleration...then the ship was infused with the energy warp that diverted it into the fourth dimension. And so into the deeps beyond Pluto, into those vast, incomprehensible spaces, the graveyard realm of comets and leftover materials from the birth of the Solar System. Then deeper into the space yawning between the edge of the Solar System and far-flung Alpha Centauri. And as yet only half of the copper block in the power unit had been consumed into atomic power.

The automatic controls functioned flawlessly, controlled by the computers that had been pre-programmed. After some four light years—as measured in the normal three-dimensional universe—had been traversed, the *Ultra* dropped back into normal space. Its speed was now the same as it had been just before the dimensional transition—a fraction below the speed of light. Then the forward rockets began firing, gradually slowing their speed before the Alpha system would be reached.

Abna stirred slowly, and immediately he did so, he felt his pulses racing as life began to surge through him. For a long moment he lay looking at the softly glowing yellow lights in the curved metal ceiling overhead, then moving his gaze he assessed the situation.

Nearby, in their sprung beds, the Amazon and Viona were also slowly recovering consciousness and, like Abna, their bodies were strained upwards now against the withholding straps. No longer was acceleration or deceleration pinning them down: that had ceased and, a constant velocity having been attained, everything had become weightless.

Moving with featherweight ease, Abna unbuckled the straps from about him and literally floated from his bed to the switchboard. Here he pressed a button and there gradually came into being the artificial gravity that made movement normal. This done, Abna moved to the observation port and gazed steadily out into space upon the great backdrop of the First Galaxy— the Milky Way—and ahead and to one side of them, so flawlessly had the course been mapped, there lay the glimmering point of Alpha Centauri. Abna looked at it for a long time, until at length he was able to determine that Alpha was not one point but two. The first evidence of its binary nature was becoming evident, which indicated their enormous distance from Earth.

"How are we making out?" Abna turned as the Amazon came to his side. rubbing her arms briskly to restore long-impeded circulation.

"Pretty well from the look of things. I haven't checked on the instruments yet, but we're plainly moving in normal space and approaching our destination."

Abna turned to the main computer, and for a moment or two busied himself with feeding readings into it. "Twenty thousand billion miles." Abna said, turning. "We are now just over four light years away from Earth. Which means we will soon be entering the Alphan system."

Viona and the Amazon nodded silently, digesting the incredible facts of their accomplishment.

"The best thing will be a meal, a check-up telescopically, and then continue onwards," Abna decided—and this was the plan they adopted.

Abna made a routine check of the power plant while the Amazon again checked the figures for the course. Everything seemed to be in order and, surprisingly enough, space ahead was completely empty of stray bodies. Even the super-radar system, flashing out to millions of miles ahead of their position, did not rebound from any object. It looked as though the remaining gulf separating them from Alpha Centauri was indeed free of all dangerous or damaging objects.

Viona took over the task of studying Alpha through the telescopic equipment, securing a view of the binary closer than any ever known before. The absolute separateness of Alpha and Proxima was now clearly marked. But this was by no means enough for Viona. She switched on the stereoscopic apparatus and studied the result intently.

"What," she asked her father, "do you make of this?"

Abna came over to her and after a momentary study of the spectro-screen he smiled in satisfaction. The most dominant color element in Alpha and Proxima was green. Bright, clear cut, emerald green.

"Copper!" Abna exclaimed. "In the gaseous state. It is therefore a foregone conclusion that any planets of Alpha must also possess copper in the solidified state. Like father, like son."

"No sign of any planets yet," Viona commented. "Probably too early to expect it, though."

CHAPTER THREE
PLANETFALL

Their observations satisfied them that they were still on course and vastly nearer Alpha and Proxima than they had formerly been.

"It gives one some idea of how enormously empty space really is," Abna said thoughtfully, loading another copper bar into the power plant. "In all the light-years we've covered, we have not encountered a single obstacle, yet to look at the heavens from Earth one would think it difficult to dodge collision...."

"Planets!" Viona gasped out excitedly. "I can see planets around the Alpha-Proxima luminary!"

The Amazon raised her head sharply from contemplating the navigation instruments.

"How many of them?"

"As near as I can tell, there are three. Two fairly close to the luminary, and one a long way out. The farthest one looks queer, somehow: misty, phosphorescent. Better take a look for yourselves."

The Amazon looked first, silently contemplating the disks of two quite clearly defined worlds bathed in the twin lights of Alpha and Proxima. At a rough estimate she decided that these worlds were probably about 180 million miles from their dual primary—twice as far as Earth from her own sun. But obviously, they would be worlds of intense heat due to the much vaster size of Alpha compared to the Earthly sun. Added to this there would be the not inconsiderable light and warmth of Proxima as well.

But that farther world was indeed strange. Either it was enveloped in highly luminous mist, or else it was indeed oddly phosphorescent in nature. It was too far away to be reflecting the light of the dual primary, therefore the glow must be something inherent in its own structure.

"Definitely a bit of a mystery," Abna admitted, when he, too, had looked. "Might make it our first port of call and see if we can decide what's the matter with it. I never saw a world like it before...."

Silent, they sat before the observation window and contemplated their goal. To each one of them there was a thrilling satisfaction in having covered 20,000 billion miles of empty space without mishap and— relatively—within a reasonable time, too.

"Have to start slowing down even further," Abna said after a while, as their still stupendous velocity caused the Alpha-Proxima system to leap nearer even as they watched it. "If we start decelerating again now, we'll be at just about the right velocity when we reach that outermost luminous world."

He moved over to the switchboard and converted the power of the replacement copper bar to the forward jets on full blast. By this means their terrific onrush was slowly but relentlessly slowed down by the opposite pressure striving to force the *Ultra* backwards as it hurtled forwards. With the passage of time, the 'braking' effect at last began to have an appreciable effect.

"It looks to me," Viona said, at the telescope as usual, "as though both those nearer worlds are populated. If not that, then they at least have something resembling cities."

The Amazon came across to the instrument and looked for herself. Under the ultra-powerful lenses the nearer planets to the binary, which appeared smudgy to the naked eye, leaped into acid-sharp prominence, revealing several things simultaneously. There was an atmosphere on each world for one thing, and indeed drifts of water vapor, which announced clouds. Beneath these clouds was a patchwork of light and dark areas, probably corresponding to continents and oceans. The main point was that the continental areas were pockmarked with square shapes interwoven with straight lines. Definitely they could not be natural formations, so the only conclusion was cities linked by roads, rails, or some other form of communication.

"Wonder if they're a backward people?" Viona asked, as her mother looked at her thoughtfully, "If they are, we'll seem like beings of wonder: If they're not, we'll probably be resented as interlopers."

"Either way, we can take care of ourselves," the Amazon replied, shrugging. Then she took over Abna's job at the control board while he, too, made a study of the scene ahead.

His interest, however, was not concentrated so much on the normal worlds as upon the luminous outermost one, toward which he presently directed the telescope. Even now, however, when they were only a few million miles from the planet, he could not detect anything beyond the uniform glowing grayness. The only problem that was resolved was that sunlight was not responsible for the glow. It was internal.

"Maybe molten," he decided finally, when Viona and the Amazon had looked.

"Maybe," the Amazon agreed. "In which case we'll give it a wide berth."

"The other possibility is radioactivity," Viona suggested. "I know that a world entirely radioactive seems a tall order, but it could happen just the same. Why don't we try the long-range Geiger-counter apparatus?"

Abna nodded and moved towards it. Switching it so that its long-range beam would directly impinge on the gray world ahead of them, he then waited for results, Viona and the Amazon to either side of him. Nor was it long before the reflected beam, operating much on the principle of radar, returned and set up a violent clicking noise.

"It *is* radioactive!" Viona gasped, surprised. "That guess of mine was dead right! Listen to the row! It must be absolutely crawling with atomic disintegration or something."

"Must be," Abna admitted soberly, switching off. "I think we'd do best to keep clear of that planet. Its emanations might conceivably pierce our neutralizing screens and cause plenty of trouble.... We'll change course and head to that world which is a shade farther from the binary than its neighbor. If there should be intelligent people, we might learn more about this distant radioactive planet."

"Evidently it isn't dangerous enough to send radioactive emanations across space to these other worlds," Viona remarked.

"Or else," the Amazon pointed out, "the people populating those worlds are not affected by radioactivity. Because our physical structure cannot stand radioactivity does not mean that theirs cannot."

There was no other way of finding out the true conditions but to land on the nearest of the two 'normal' planets, and to this end Abna again took control of the switches, still cutting down the speed of the *Ultra* until after a long interval it had dropped from its former velocity to a trifling 10,000 miles an hour. It was when this 'crawl' had been achieved that the outermost layer of the nearest planet's atmosphere was also contacted.

Still Abna cut down the velocity, leveling the huge machine out so it was finally flying parallel to the surface of this infinitely far-flung world. Intently, the Amazon and Viona gazed below, their view only momentarily obscured by cloud drifts. They could descry—as they had in space through the telescope—quite normal-looking continents and oceans, the former laced with what were plainly cities of gray-colored metal. Streets and terraces there were in abundance, but nowhere a sign of a pedestrian or traffic level, as on Earth. No moving vehicles. No aircraft or space ships. Only this waste of gray-colored buildings, becoming larger as the *Ultra* swept lower.

Finally Abna selected clear ground beyond one of the cities and brought the *Ultra* down with scarcely a jar. Switches clicked in rapid succession and the soft humming of the power plant ceased. The silence seemed, for a moment, incredible.

"Twenty thousand billion miles and not a hitch!" the Amazon exclaimed, giving a triumphant glance.

"Notice the double shadows everywhere?" Abna asked, peering outside. "Result of two suns close together."

Viona and the Amazon nodded together. Through the observation window there was a wilderness of barren rock, slate-gray in color, and all of it brightly illuminated by the double suns. Angling her head against the window, Viona peered upward and then blinked. For a moment she caught a glimpse of the blazing circle which was Alpha Centauri, appearing about twice as large and twice as bright as the sun seen from Earth, whilst to the left of this torrid giant there was a smaller sun, intense blue white, and adding to the intense heat which must be outside the *Ultra*. Within it, the insulated walls kept everything at normal temperature.

"I suppose—there must be people?" Abna hesitated over the question as he surveyed the empty pale blue sky. "We didn't see anybody."

"Nor vehicles or aircraft," Viona added. "Be just too bad if we've come to a dead world."

"Most sensible thing is to see what kind of a world it is and then decide our course of action," the Amazon said, and with that she turned to the instruments that gave direct contact with the exterior.

"Atmosphere is breathable enough," she announced at length. "Fairly high preponderance of hydrogen, but that should not worry us. Traces, too, of copper gas in a highly volatile condition, which augurs well for supplies of copper for the power plant. Atmospheric pressure eighteen pounds to the square inch, which isn't too much different from our own fourteen. Humidity sixty-five percent, which will prove pretty clammy. Temperature 130 degrees F. Gravity similar to Earth, or as near as makes no difference...."

"In fact, a world quite able to support our type of life," Abna said. "What do we do, then? Fly around it and see what there is?"

"No point in doing that." the Amazon responded. "We've seen it is a world of almost equal division of continents and oceans, and just where we are now there is a city close by. Best thing to do is arm ourselves and start exploring"

"Why not try the radio?" Viona suggested. "Even if we don't understand the language, we'll be able to tell if there's anybody alive. Surely a civilization worth anything has radio developed as one of its sciences?"

Without waiting for her mother or father to reply,

she tuned in the radio equipment arid stood listening. Then she frowned in vague disbelief. There was not the faintest whisper. Only a crackling of static, probably engendered by the mighty sun and far-off radioactive planet. Certainly there were no voices or anything resembling music.

"No need to look so disappointed." Abna commented. "If anybody had landed on Earth in the Middle Ages, they would not have heard radio, either: I'm beginning to hope that we really have landed on a world where science is not very well developed. We'll be able to teach them something."

CHAPTER FOUR
HYPNOSIS

Abna opened the nearby weapon locker and took out three powerful disintegrator guns. Viona and the Amazon took one each and Abna himself retained the third; then he pressed the button that caused the airlock to unfasten itself and open slowly. When it had swung to its limit and clicked into position, there came drifting into the control room the air of this far-away world—heavy, overpoweringly hot. It was as though somebody had opened a furnace door a dozen yards away.

With the eager impetuosity of youth, Viona took a flying leap through the open airlock and landed gracefully outside. Immediately she gasped a little as the roasting heat of the dual suns beat down upon her.

"I don't think we'll need sun-helmets," the Amazon said, alighting beside her. "According to the instruments these suns emit little or no ultraviolet, and that is the main cause of our Earthly troubles in direct sunlight. Hot, yes—but not dangerous."

Hot was an understatement, as they soon discovered. Here indeed was a torrid world, and before they had covered half a mile all three were perspiring freely and, strong though they were, their footsteps began to labor.

"At least there is one advantage," the Amazon said presently, withdrawing one of her detector instruments from her belt. "This planet has a revolution of 22 hours, 14 minutes, Earth-time, which means we'll get a bit of relief when night comes. Since it seems to be mainly cloudless here, we should get a rapid radiation of heat from the surface and comparative cold."

Viona and Abna did not comment. It was nearly too hot to think, never mind talk. They kept on plodding steadily, the Amazon in the center, and after what seemed an age of grilling advance they reached the end of the brief plateau where the *Ultra* had landed and they had before them a clear view of one of the many cities they had seen.

The first thing that impressed them was its simplicity of design. All of the buildings, and there were hundreds of them, were identical—blocks of them split up by streets at intervals. In the few open spaces there were park-like areas in which grew drab, dusty-looking vegetation, utterly unlike anything known on Earth or her neighboring worlds. Every building had a ground floor only—no upper storey, and each one possessed one window—without glass—and one door.

"I don't know what you think," Abna remarked at length, as they stood surveying, "but it looks to me like a vast penitentiary, or something. Everything is so absolutely identical. Just like a prison, or army barracks, or something...."

"Look!" the Amazon said abruptly, pointing.

Her attention, and now that of Abna arid Viona, was centered upon a long file of moving figures. There were probably a hundred of them, marching slowly and yet with the clockwork precision of robots. Instantly Viona whipped powerful binoculars from her shoulder and focussed them quickly.

"I'll be a comet's tail!" she exclaimed, startled. "Scientific law says that no two planets can evolve identical beings, but it's happened here! Those folks are indistinguishable from Earthlings!"

By this time her mother and father were also gazing intently, and there was no gainsaying the truth of Viona's statement. The beings of this world looked like Earth men and women—even to their faces. They were all attired in identical clothing, a kind of dull gray, one-piece uniform that covered them from neck to ankles. Each also wore a round hat, most of them smeared with dirt. Upon each face was the indelible impress of depression, unresolved hopes, of bitter frustration

"Cheerful-looking gang," Abna commented at length, lowering the glasses. "From the way they march and the identical uniforms, I'd say they're prisoners of some sort. Maybe my guess was not far wrong when I said this place might be a penitentiary."

The Amazon and Viona did not reply. They watched the file of men and women until buildings hid them from sight, then they put their glasses away.

"To me," the Amazon said, frowning, "this doesn't make sense! They must have seen the *Ultra* descending: If not that, they must have heard it. Why doesn't somebody come to investigate?"

"If those folks are prisoners they perhaps can't," Viona replied.

"Then why don't their guards? There must be somebody who is curious about our arrival, surely?"

Apparently there was not, for as the three remained where they were for a while there was no evidence of an investigating party coming down the long road which led from the city to the plateau.

"Well?" Abna asked at length. "Do we investigate now or wait for the night to descend and so cloak our movements?"

"We investigate now," the Amazon decided. "We have weapons powerful enough to take care of us, and the sooner we know the kind of world we've come to, the better."

So they advanced again, moving with more caution when at length they had covered the distance of the main city road and had the drab metallic buildings all around them. The file of men and women they had seen had completely disappeared.

"Queerest place ever!" Viona declared, hands on hips as she gazed about her. "If those people were prisoners, or slaves, or something, why isn't there some evidence of the place where they are employed? And why are there no guards to keep watch? The whole thing's cockeyed."

"Then we'll soon have a chance to solve it, perhaps," the Amazon said, cocking her gun in readiness. "Take a look at what is coming."

Viona and Abna saw immediately what she meant. Some distance ahead of them another file of men and women were emerging from a huge manhole opening in the street itself, coming up from below. Still with that same clocklike precision, the uniformed men and women marched and, grimly ready, the three from Earth waited for some kind of action.

None was forthcoming, on either side. Little by little the file of workers broke up and into each dwelling went either a man or a woman, closing the door after them. The fact that the three wanderers from afar were in full view, guns leveled, did not seem to make any difference. There was not even a glance in their direction.... And at last the street was empty again.

"Beyond me," Viona sighed, putting her gun back in its holster. "Unless maybe they're all blind—perhaps from the glare of the twin suns."

"Possible, but unlikely," the Amazon said. "I hardly think you are correct, Viona, because they walk too accurately for sightless people. No, it looks to me more like a case of deep hypnotism. The strangely mechanical walking, the disregard of everything around them. Let's see what we have along those lines."

Again from her golden instrument belt she took a finely balanced detector with an atomic-powered core. Switching it into commission, she watched the delicate needle intently as it oscillated gently and then, very gradually it began to rise on its universally mounted pivot until it was pointing straight up—or rather on a slight deviation from the vertical.

"And what does that signify?" Abna asked, puzzled.

"It means that my guess was right. Hypnotic power, of almost unbelievable intensity, is behind all this. And the source of it is where this needle is pointing."

Viona and Abna shaded their eyes from the savage glare and gazed into the cloudless sky. Nothing significant was visible.

"That radioactive planet maybe?" Viona asked suddenly, transferring her attention back to her mother.

The Amazon shook her head. She was now studying another of the instruments, a small version of the long range Geiger-counter apparatus aboard the *Ultra*.

"No, Viona, that doesn't fit," she said finally. "That radioactive world is so far away that its radioactivity does not affect this planet in the least, and therefore hypnotic power from the same source could not reach this far either. The more likely proposition is the neighbor world to this one, situated maybe twenty million miles off, about half as far as Mars is from Earth at its nearest point."

"But it's incredible!" Viona protested. "Think of the power needed to enforce hypnosis over that distance!"

"That is just what I am thinking about." The Amazon put her instrument back in place and reflected. Then: "The whole situation is paradoxical. Here we have a world that seems so backward that even radio isn't used, yet twenty million miles or so distant there is a hypnotic source, clearly shown by the mental vibrations on our detector. They are of an incredibly high order. Against that we must remember that this system may be highly atomic, as evidenced by that single outer world which is a seething cauldron of radioactivity. If atomic power is as cheap as water on that neighbor world, then maybe their hypnotic amplification is achieved by that means. Otherwise it leaves us with an amazing possibility."

"Which is?" Abna asked.

"A planet that is in itself...a brain!"

Viona dabbed her fingertips at a trickle of perspiration as it coursed down her nose, then she smiled.

"A whole planet converted into a brain!" she exclaimed. "I can imagine anything but that. Planetary matter is inanimate. It cannot possibly become a thinking, reasoning medium."

"Human beings—living things—are also inanimate at root, yet they have the apparatus, the ganglia, and neurones within them to render thinking possible. As I see it, any material structure might develop the power of mental transmission and conception...." The Amazon paused and smiled wryly: "Yes, maybe I am getting a bit ahead of myself, but it's either that, or atomic power concentrated to the limit. Nothing else can explain such tremendous influence over such a distance. Whatever it is which is exerting hypnosis is not of this world but right outside it."

"And yet we do not come under it," Abna pointed out, at which the Amazon looked passing surprised.

"No, that is true. The answer to that might be that our brain structure differs from that of the men and women we have seen and therefore we're not affected. In any case, the simplest way to find out what it happening is to try to question one of these slaves. Even use apparatus of our own to neutralize the hypnotic force for a while, and allow one of these people to have their own individuality."

"Right!" Abna agreed promptly, and pointed to the closed door of the nearest dwelling. "We'll take that one."

He strode across to it and, pulling out his gun, hammered with the butt upon the solid metal portal. Nothing happened, even though the trio had seen a woman go inside only a few minutes before.

"Only one answer," the Amazon decided, and with that she withdrew slightly, then moved forward at a run and crashed her right shoulder into the portal with all her strength. Under the impact the metal lock snapped and precipitated her into a dimly lighted room.

CHAPTER FIVE
WOMAN OF AXILON

She looked about her. The dimness of the room was caused by a shade having been drawn three-quarters the length of the main window, thereby reducing the sunlight to a subdued glimmer. The room itself was obviously a sleeping chamber. A very earthly looking bed lay diagonal to the window, and there was a queerly fashioned chair and an object with apparently collapsible cupboards.

In the bed lay the silently sleeping figure of a woman. She had removed her uniform now and lay under a single covering like a sheet, her attire a loose-fitting sleeveless garment closed with an ornament at the throat.

"Must be the sleep of the dead," Abna commented, coming to the Amazon's side. "You'd think the noise alone as we came in would have awakened her."

"Not if the sleep is basically hypnotic, which it probably is." From her belt the Amazon removed an object rather like a small-scale projector and carefully adjusted it. When she had it to her liking she added, "This ought to neutralize the hypnotic influence, at least for a time. It emits a disturbing electrical field which should be enough to upset the control over this woman's brain."

A faint amber beam glowed from the instrument as the Amazon switched it on.

Whilst she kept the beam playing about the woman's head, Viona shook her gently. And at last she stirred and looked dazedly around her with eyes of very dark blue. As she finally realized that three strangers were gazing down on her, she drew back quickly towards the bed head, her whole attitude one of intense fear.

"We have no wish to harm you," the Amazon said quietly, keeping the beam trained.

A volley of words broke from the woman's lips, but her language made no sense whatever—at least not to the Amazon and Viona. Abna for his part drew down his brows and then closed his eyes in concentration. Neither the Amazon nor Viona disturbed him, knowing that under stress he could assimilate an entire language by concentrating upon the mind of the person uttering it. And so it proved to be in this case, for when the woman's outburst had ceased, he reopened his eyes and smiled at her, laying a huge, protecting hand upon her shoulder. He spoke a few words in her own tongue, and that brought a smile of relief to the woman's face.

"What's going on?" the Amazon asked, irritated that in this instance Abna's power was in excess of her own.

"Until I reassured her," Abna explained, "she believed that we had come from the Masters and were about to punish her with death for some crime or other. She knows now that we are friends. As far as I can tell, she is an extremely frightened, subjugated woman."

"That's obvious from her expression," the Amazon said. "Find out what else there is—what she and her fellow-workers are doing, and who the Masters are."

"Exactly what I intend to do." Abna turned back to the woman and began to converse with her, long and earnestly. Throughout the time the Amazon kept the neutralizing beam in action, and at the same time noted the various expressions on the faces of both the woman and Abna. Finally Abna relaxed and looked thoughtful. The woman was by now sitting up in the bed, looking from one to the other in silent wonderment.

"Well?" Viona prompted finally, and Abna gave a little start.

"Sorry; I was just thinking out what Ilosa has been telling me. It seems that this world is fairly well populated by men and women who look surprisingly like us. The answer to their parallel physique seems to lie in the planetary conditions—for except for the excessive heat, this world is very similar to Earth in all other respects, therefore it produces a similar type of life. The surprising thing is that these people know little or nothing about scientific things, and because of that they are absolute slaves to the Mizanu. Freely interpreted, that means the Masters."

"Who reside on that neighbor world?" the Amazon asked.

"Apparently, yes. I say 'apparently' because Ilosa

doesn't seem too sure about it. She only knows, like the rest of her people, that there is a dominant power on the neighbor world which influences the actions of the people here. On this world there is no social life, no relaxation—no anything except work and bed, and finally the grave.

"They are born, marry, and die in captivity. More often than not whole families are split apart by the whim of the Masters as certain workers are drafted off to new regions."

"And at what are they working? Something underground?"

"Hard to decide," Abna replied. "Since Ilosa has no knowledge of scientific terms, she cannot clearly express what she means. My guess from her description of her work is that she and the rest of them are getting radioactive materials together for some purpose or other. Probably for the Masters."

The Amazon reflected as she studied the woman. "In that case these people are either immune to radioactivity, or else they must wear insulated clothes when at work. There'd be signs of burning somewhere otherwise, and this woman's flesh is apparently unmarked."

"We can only find that out by seeing where they work," Viona said. "And by that I mean join them."

"And what good would that do?" the Amazon demanded. "From the look of things, our task is to visit the Masters and find out the reason for their ruthless behavior. It's plain that they have a profound knowledge of science even if these luckless people have not."

"True enough," Viona admitted, "but I still think it might benefit us to see how these people work and what it is they're doing. We'll be able to work with complete, freedom because the hypnosis does not affect us."

The Amazon glanced at Abna. "Ask her if the hypnosis is ever lifted long enough for them to become possessors of their own individualities."

Abna complied and the woman immediately answered, at considerable length.

"It seems," Abna announced finally, "that the hypnosis is a permanent thing, but sometimes it is in less strength than others, during which time the victims—Ilosa among them—gain some glimpse of their real personalities and taste the very edge of freedom. Then the hypnosis clamps down again and they are powerless to exert their own wills. They are all the time conscious of their own personalities, but are powerless to exert them. Body and soul, they are the slaves of the Mizanu."

"A state of affairs which needs rectifying," the Amazon decided. "Our policy is to help the backward scientific races, and free those who are oppressed so that they can be drawn eventually into one grand universal brotherhood. This world seems like an excellent one on which to start."

"Its name is Axilon," Abna said. "Near as I can interpret it, anyhow."

"You have told this woman who we are, and our purpose?" Viona inquired.

"I have, and she is more than grateful that there

appears at last to be a possibility of securing freedom. It appears, incidentally, that punishment of the unruly ones takes the form of banishment to Nur, that radio-active world we saw. Once there, death of the most anguishing kind is inevitable...."

"And that," the Amazon mused, "seems to suggest that the Masters have some means of knowing how their planet of slaves are behaving. Maybe long-range telescopes or television, and radio pick-ups for sound."

"I don't think so," Abna said. "Unless this woman is incapable of explaining such things. I lean to the view that the guards do all the watching and reporting back to the Masters. Apparently, there are quite a lot of them underground, supervising—all men, entirely unaffected by the hypnosis."

"Unaffected by it?" The Amazon looked surprised. "That seems strange."

"Not altogether. The physique of the guards is different from that of the slaves. Apparently they belong to the Masters' world, and are of a totally different physical structure altogether. Presumably their brains, too, are unaffected by hypnosis just as ours are. It is only these unfortunate people who are the sufferers."

There was a long silence, then the Amazon glanced at Viona.

"Yes, Viona, I think you had the right idea," she admitted. "We must go amongst these people and see what we can do to lighten the load for them. By that means we can probably find out more concerning the Masters before we deal with them directly. Ask this woman, Abna, if she has any spare uniforms—though I doubt, even if she has, that there will be any to fit you."

Abna turned to the woman again and questioned her. From the vigorous nodding of her head added to the alien words, it seemed evident that the answer was affirmative.

"She has half a dozen," Abna said at length. "They are kept as spares for when the others are too thread-bare. The fortunate thing is that the material is capable of being stretched and staying that way. By that means, workers of all sizes are constantly fitted by starting with a basic small garment. So maybe I'll get away with it."

"Only partly, I'm afraid," Viona said anxiously. "Your main trouble is being so tall. One of the guards somewhere is sure to remember he has not seen a man of your dimensions before—then we'll be in a mess."

"No reason why we should be," Abna smiled. "I'll go back to the *Ultra* and use the Decreaser. That will solve the difficulty. By narrowing the electronic orbits of the atoms of my body I can remove as much bulk as I desire. I'll return as a five-foot-sixer or something like it."

"You do that," the Amazon assented. "Meanwhile Viona and I will get into our uniforms, and then do what we can to understand this woman's language."

"And if you don't succeed in that," Abna remarked, reaching the doorway, "I'll transfer it mentally to you when I return."

CHAPTER SIX
THE DEVIL'S WORKSHOP

By this time the woman Ilosa, obviously realizing that she had indeed found friends, looked at the Amazon and Viona expectantly. And thereupon, still keeping the neutralizing beam steadily trained, the Amazon set out to learn the rudiments of the alien language and fill in the blanks for herself. Her main reason, though she did not admit it openly, was to prove that mental mastery was not entirely Abna's prerogative.... For all that, she failed in her objective, for she was no wiser by the time Abna had returned— And the change in him was extraordinary. He stood no more than five feet six, not as tall as the Amazon.

"This," Abna said, as the two women stared at him in amazement, "is what must be meant by 'coming down in the world.' Let me have one of those uniforms, please."

Viona handed him one, and he began to scramble into it, asking a question as he did so: "Get any further with the language?"

"No," the Amazon confessed, rather bitterly. "We'll have to rely on you after all."

"Too bad," Abna grinned. "All right—here it is...."

He relaxed for a moment in fastening up the uniform and his face became an intent mask of concentration. In those few seconds, as they attuned their minds to receive the incoming thought-waves, both women sensed in completeness the entire language of this world of Axilon. To them it was a thing of wonder to have the knowledge of a complicated tongue so easily transferred; to Abna merely an effort of concentration, since he admitted no barrier to the power of thought.

"Got it?" he inquired at length, relaxing.

"Yes," the Amazon assented. "I think we—"

She paused and stood listening, as across the silences of the slave world there suddenly came the rising and falling note of a powerful siren. It sounded to be an infinite distance away—unless, as was probable, it was underground.

"That a warning or what?" the Amazon asked Ilosa sharply.

"Beginning of the work period," the woman replied, grimacing.

"So soon! But you have barely been off duty for an hour!"

"I know. That is how the shifts are controlled here. Two hours on and one hour off—constantly."

"Cut out that neutralizing beam," Abna ordered quickly. "We want to see what happens—and hurry up and get into your uniforms."

Both women did as they were told and, with the cutting off of the neutralization, Ilosa relaxed for a moment, a look of total blankness creeping over her face as her individuality was utterly overpowered by the overwhelming hypnosis of the neighbor world. Abna looked at her intently, his face grim.

"This influence is certainly very thorough," be commented, as the Amazon fastened up the neck of her uniform. "I'm even commencing to lean toward your idea of an entire planetary brain."

There was no time to pursue the theory, for at that moment the woman rose from her bed, reached for her uniform, and then slipped one shoulder from her night-attire. Abna turned his back. In all directions doors were opening and shutting as men and women slaves left their domiciles and slowly began to form into a file, similar to the one they had originally made when emerging from the depths.

"All right, father, you can look now," Viona said at length.

Abna turned, beholding Ilosa in her uniform, her eyes now completely expressionless.

"This is our chance," Abna said. "No guards are in sight, far as I can see, and these folks are too hypno-tized to know that others are among them."

He ushered the Amazon and Viona out quickly as he spoke, and then slammed the door as he, too, stepped out into the street. In another moment all three of them had taken up their positions amongst the workers, by whom they were completely disregarded. Then, pres-ently, when others had arrived, the file got on the move, evidently directed by hypnotic influence.

The great manhole opening in the street center was reached. Having descended into it, the three from Earth looked about them interestedly as they continued the downward march. They were obviously descending a man-made slope cut into the rocks, and lighted by long tubes of brilliance that had a vague relationship to neon gas.

The slope continued downward for perhaps half a mile and ended at a mighty metal door. Here the file stopped automatically and waited. In a few moments the door opened and from beyond it there came a gush of air that was overpoweringly hot even in this torrid land.

"Workshops or laboratories of some kind," the Amazon murmured.

The file moved forward again into this area of intense industry, and in twos and threes the men and women departed to pre-appointed tasks, finally leaving Abna, the Amazon, and Viona standing together.

Abna murmured, "We'd better pretend to be doing something before we're spotted. That machine over there; we can make believe we're attending to it."

They all moved to a mass of equipment, which resembled a huge generator. Its purpose they did not understand, but they made a convincing show of operating its controls.

To all intents and purposes this was a gigantic engineering workshop, a mighty foundry with all manner of incomprehensible machines since, of course, the engineering of Axilon was utterly at variance with that of Earth.

Then, after a while, they beheld the first of the guards, presumably a denizen of the neighbor world of the Mizanu. In height he was about five feet and his width seemed almost the same. His gross body was topped by a round bullet-head and brutal-featured face.

"The puzzle to me," Abna remarked, studying the guard covertly as he continued 'working' on the mystery apparatus, "is how any of his race could ever have become intelligent enough to devise hypnosis."

"Who says they ever did?" Viona murmured. "Obviously he's not the intelligent type. He would probably be classed with the apes back on Earth, whereas Man represents the Intelligentsia. Nobody will ever convince me that a creature like him could be intelligent...."

"It looks," the Amazon said, "as though he has noticed us. Better be ready for anything."

The guard would have investigated matters had not his attention been suddenly distracted by a piercing scream of anguish. He immediately swung toward the source of the sound, and the Amazon, Viona, and Abna looked up quickly, too. They saw a woman, screaming with pain, flesh blistering and corroding upon her right shoulder. At this point her uniform had been burned completely through, and the effect was as though molten lead had been poured on her. She staggered and fell.

Immediately half a dozen workers deserted their tasks to go to her aid—but before she could be reached, the guards converged inwards.

"What's going on?" Viona asked quickly, intently watching.

"That woman has been burned by radioactive material of some kind," the Amazon answered. "I'd know that kind of burn anywhere. The trouble is we don't know in this alien set-up which things are radioactive and which not—"

"Those other workers moved to help her," Abna pointed out. "Queer thing that, if they're constantly hypnotized."

"Not altogether." The Amazon was still watching the scene and listening to the groans of the stricken woman. "Reaction to danger, the sudden need to help one of their own kind in distress. Those inner instincts cannot be overcome by hypnotism, any more than can the natural functions of the body."

"To your work, the lot of you!" bellowed the voice of one of the guards, using the Axilonian language.

Some of the workers obeyed; others hesitated. It was plain they were struggling between mental compulsion and their own faintly awakened personalities. Then one of them moved forward quickly and, disregarding the leveled weapons of the guards, began to do his best to raise the injured woman from the floor. For his reward he received a stream of fire from the nearest flame gun, the searing beam slicing across his back. With a gasping cry he fell across the woman he had been striving to help.

"To work!" came the repeated order. "And quickly!

You men—get these two out of the way and replace them."

"I don't like this sort of thing a bit," Abna muttered, his fists clenched. "These poor devils simply don't stand a chance."

The Amazon deserted her work and moved forward quickly, reaching the guard whose flame-gun had incapacitated a would-be rescuer. Hearing her behind him, he turned sharply and leveled his weapon.

The Amazon catapulted herself forward, hands outthrust. Her fingers clamped on the guard's thick, muscular neck just as he was about to fire.

The gun jolted out of his hand. Then he was on the floor with merciless fingers closing about his throat. At the back of his mind was a dim bewilderment that such a thing could happen; a worker who could revolt was unknown—until now—and the strength for a female was unbelievable.

The other guards whipped their guns from their holsters. That was the signal for Viona to hurtle across the intervening space and close with two of the guards simultaneously, her bent-in arms dragging relentlessly on the necks of the men to either side of her, and all the efforts of the two she had pinned failed to dislodge her from between them.

In this area one guard was left. He kneeled, sighting his gun and waiting for a good opportunity. Instead a fist with the impact of a trip-hammer crashed down on the back of his neck and flattened him to the floor. Abna lifted the heavy body by the belt, then flung it a dozen yards across the workroom. Like a ridiculous rag doll it struck one of the instruments, bounced back, and then became motionless.

After which Viona found the going easier. One of the guards she was pinning down was snatched away from her. Abna had only to slam up his fist with withering force to smash the guard's jaw to pulp and drop him in his tracks. By the time he had done this, he found Viona settling her own victim. He lay on his face, her knees in the small of his back and her right forearm locked under his chin. It was only a matter of moments before Viona's inexorable upward pressure broke the guard's spine. He relaxed, dead.

Abna said, "Now we'd better fix up these two."

The two women, still breathing hard from their efforts, watched as he went on his knees beside the injured man and woman. Both of them were still conscious but obviously in considerable pain. Abna made no attempt to help them up: instead he remained beside them, his eyes shut, his forehead wrinkled with concentration. What happened afterwards was nothing new to the Amazon and Viona: they had seen these miracle feats of mind over matter often before. And so it was again. By degrees the torn, burned flesh on the shoulder of the woman and the back of the man began to heal, and with the process the lines of anguish vanished from their faces and they became wondering and half afraid instead.

Presently Abna opened his eyes and smiled, getting to his feet.

"Better?" he inquired, in their own language, and helped them to rise.

They did not answer: they only stared.

The reason was plain. With the cessation of physical pain, which had overridden the hypnosis normally controlling them, they had again relaxed into the mesmerism.

Completely healed of their burns, even though the torn gaps on their uniforms remained, they returned stiffly to their work.

"Now what?" the Amazon asked. "Having worked your mind-over-matter act and put them right, how much better off are we?"

"We're not," Abna shrugged. "Indeed, everything we've done has probably been seen and noted down by the Mizanu. But at least we have tipped the balance of power somewhat in our direction. For the first time in history, probably, there has been a small-scale revolution in this devil's workshop."

He looked about him and then continued: "This is quite the most inhuman set-up I've ever struck! Several of these machines are dealing with radioactive ores, and these workers have no protection whatever against accidents. Presumably, it doesn't signify if several of them get killed: there are always others to take their place."

The two women looked about them, still as puzzled as they had ever been regarding the nature of this giant workshop. Everybody was busy—some on radioactive equipment; others on the construction of incomprehensible apparatus; and yet others were building what could have been small space machines.

"The purpose of it all?" There was complete bafflement in the Amazon's voice. "What is the motive behind all this, I wonder?"

"That's up to the Mizanu to explain," Viona responded. "And the sooner we tackle the source, in the shape of that neighbor world, the better—"

Then guards from the further reaches of the workshop appeared.

"We have our own weapons under these uniforms," the Amazon said. "Why don't we use them? They're superior to heat guns."

Abna shook his head. "Better to use evading tactics and muscular strength."

He prepared for action as the guards came nearer, but they stopped when they reached the complicated machine where Ilosa was working. Before she realized what had happened she was whirled around and forced into the guards' midst, guns trained menacingly upon her.

Intently, the three from Earth remained motionless, watching. They expected some kind of villainy when the guard nearest Ilosa pulled an object like a torch from his tunic and leveled it at her—but the result proved it was an instrument which neutralized the hypnotic influence. In design it was probably similar to the device the Amazon herself possessed.

"We have received a report that you have been befriended by three unknowns from another world," the guard said. "Are these the three?"

The trio stood their ground as the guard glanced toward them. It was perfectly plain now that the Masters knew everything that had been happening and, by radio, had transferred the information to their brutal watchdogs on this unfortunate slave planet.

"I have nothing to say!" Ilosa's voice was defiant but tremulous.

The guard shrugged. "That is a matter of indifference to us because we know the facts. You could lighten the sentence against yourself by admitting your complicity with these three aliens who have already killed four of our numbers."

The trio glanced at one another. Around them the workers were still mechanically occupied at their tasks. Ilosa gave a beseeching look, which changed to one of sheer terror as she saw the guard beside her taking a long needle-like object from his belt.

"The Mizanu prefer complete confession before sentence," the guard explained. "If you will not give it voluntarily, you must be made to. You will, of course, be aware of the painful nature of this fluid when it enters your bloodstream."

"You can put that thing away," Abna said, moving forward. "The girl doesn't need to confess anything. We befriended this worker because she needed it. She didn't ask for it."

"Aliens," the guard said coldly, "are not welcome on Axilon, and those who frequent with them merit the death penalty."

"Nobody's going to get the death penalty while we're here," Abna said.

"Where are you from?"

"Earth. A world so far away you could never reach it even in thirty lifetimes."

"The Mizanu could," the guard retorted. "And no doubt will. It is interesting to know of this distant world which breeds braggarts and interlopers."

Abna only smiled, supreme in his knowledge of his own power. The guard glared at him and then motioned his fellows. They closed in quickly.

"It would seem," Abna remarked, gazing at the grim faces, "that the only sensible course for the slaves of this world is to stage a revolution against the brutality and hypnosis of their rulers. To that end we of Earth are dedicated, and it will take more than the Mizanu to stop us!"

The guard gave a bitter smile, which only made his face more ugly than ever.

"For your own sake, man of Earth, you had better know that the Mizanu is unconquerable. Who is there who can defy the massed power of an entire planetary brain? A brain that knows all? A world that is nothing more than thinking ganglia and cells. You would have the affront to try to defy that?"

The Amazon gave a quick, triumphant glance. Her theory that the neighbor world was a brain in itself had evidently been absolutely correct.

CHAPTER SEVEN
REVOLUTION

Ilosa spoke—hurriedly and nervously. "It is not right that these aliens should suffer for—"

She got no further than this. The guard lashed out his fist and knocked her spinning—but she had hardly touched the floor before he found himself whirled in the air and held at shoulder level by Abna's steel-strong arm.

Lowering the guard to the floor but maintaining his grip upon him, he said: "I shall now question you, also using you as a shield in case your colleagues here get restive. They cannot attack me with those guns without attacking you. The first question is, what brought the Mizanu into being?"

"I am not allowed to say," the guard panted.

"Then you must be made to. That needle-instrument looked most efficient, so I think we'll—"

"I'll tell you!" the guard interrupted hastily. "The Mizanu is one scientist of planetary dimensions."

"Explain it more clearly!" Abna snapped.

The guard breathed hard and looked desperately at his comrades. But, though their guns were ready, they dared not use them. They were so positioned that between them and Abna was the hapless guard.

"Hurry up!" Abna ordered, giving a violent shake.

"Generations ago there was a master scientist— He experimented in the field of mental control and, unintentionally, wiped out his entire race by a supreme blast of mental power. Only he was left. His brain, affected by radioactivity from the planet Nur, over-whelmed the structure of his body and grew to vast proportions. The elements of the neighbor world are such that physical structure can mate with the cellular rocks. Hence the body of the master mental-scientist withered, but his brain continued to live. It grew upon itself and finally became the planet itself—a vast, over-whelmingly powerful thinking machine."

"Yes, that's biologically possible," the Amazon said. "The neighbor world must have exactly the right elements to nurture cells. The only problem is how they remain stimulated. Possibly radioactivity from Nur is responsible for that."

"And what is the purpose of the Brain?" Abna demanded. "What are all these slaves for? What are they doing?"

The guard did not hesitate over his answer. "The Mizanu knows it is so powerful it cannot be destroyed, therefore it intends in time to bend the System to its will—even the Universe itself. There exists the possi-bility of other planetary brains in the deeps of space, and it is these that must be vanquished so there will be no opposition. To this end, to investigate the possibility of such worlds, the Mizanu sends forth emissaries. Upon what happens to them the Mizanu bases his plans."

"In other words, the slaves of this world are sent to other unknown planets to test the conditions? If they come back unharmed the Mizanu plots further. If they don't, then they are written off? In other words, they are what we of Earth call white mice?"

"They are experimental explorers," the guard said.

"And what has all this equipment to do with it?" the Amazon questioned.

"In these workshops, under the direction of the Mlianu, the special instruments for the experimental explorers are made. On the instruments is registered everything they encounter for the Mizanu to study at leisure. Apart from that, the spaceships are constructed, the electrical equipment, and everything else."

"Altogether, a very nice plan—for the Mizanu," Abna commented slowly. "Having absolute power over these slaves, he can order them to do exactly as he wishes—but that his power is not invincible is proven by the fact that I and my Earth colleagues are not affected, and neither are any of you guards. Obviously, only certain types of brains fall under the sway of the Mizanu. For that reason his dream of an ultimate Universal conquest is doomed to failure...."

"Presumably," the Amazon said, looking at the guard, "the Mizanu has some means of seeing and hearing exactly what is going on in this world?"

"The Mizanu knows everything!"

"So do you, probably," Abna said thoughtfully. "It is plain from that neutralizing instrument of yours that you know how to make the hypnosis inoperative when necessary. I venture to think you will also know where there are bigger neutralizing instruments for use in an emergency."

A startled expression crossed the guard's face; then it set again in stubborn lines. His comrades began to drift nearer, still awaiting an opportunity to use their weapons. Abna saw their intentions quite clearly, however, and drew the guard more tightly against him.

"Take me to the nearest neutralizing machine!" Abna ordered, but the guard only shook his head.

"I know where the machine is you want," Ilosa exclaimed eagerly. She had risen from the floor and came forward as she spoke. "It was used once for mass suppression of hypnosis when a worker came under suspicion and all of us had to be mentally freed in order to ask questions."

"Do you know how to operate it?" Abna asked quickly.

"I—I think so. There is only one main control switch."

"Go to it then and switch it on. I want every worker here to be master of his—and her—own will."

Immediately Ilosa got on the move and Abna stood watching her. Indeed, his attention was so much fixed upon her he forgot for the moment the extreme precariousness of his own position. One of the nearer guards immediately saw his chance and brought up his gun.

He had reckoned, however, without the lightning wits and speed of the Amazon. She noticed the gun start to rise and her action was instantaneous. Regardless of the fact that the other guns could deal with her she sprang forward, knocking up the guard's gun arm and deflecting the deadly beam into the lofty roof. Then with hardly a second's pause she delivered a smashing left-hander that sent the guard collapsing amidst his fellows. They, just about to fire their own weapons, were bowled over with their comrade and by the time they had sorted themselves out, the Amazon had wrenched out her gun from under her tunic.

"Many thanks," Abna said briefly, glancing at her. "Serves me right for not keeping my eyes open."

The Amazon did not answer. She kept her gun steady, and in a moment or two, likewise armed, Viona came to her side. The guards got to their feet, but they made no moves to try to reverse the situation. It had been driven into them by this time that these three from the distant Earth were not to be trifled with.

The workers who had been so disinterested in the situation around them began to cease work and rub their foreheads gently. Turning, they looked around them—first at the distant Ilosa, who was operating the hypnosis-neutralization machine; then at Abna, the Amazon, and Viona, with the luckless head guard in their midst.

"Earthman, you are a fool!" the guard panted, swinging round in Abna's grip. "Each worker here has now been released from hypnotic control and the

Mizanu will be fully aware of it. His reprisal will be instantaneous and devastating!"

"I doubt it," Abna answered coldly. "These slaves are of considerable value to him and mass extermination wouldn't suit his ends at all. In any case it doesn't signify, because these workers are going to fight for themselves from here on—"

"That depends on how long the influence of that machine lasts, doesn't it?" the Amazon asked.

"Since it is presumably powered atomically, like everything else in this place, I can't foresee an early end to the neutralization," Abna replied. "And talking of atomic power reminds me...."

He turned again to the guard and shook him savagely. "For what reason does the Mizanu need radioactives?"

"To the Mizanu they are food," the guard answered, and it was plain he was scared at having to make the admission. "The Mizanu lives by the power of Nur, but there may come a time when Nur ceases to pour forth his radio-energy. When that happens, the Mizanu must have another source of nourishment—so certain members of the Axilonian race do nothing else but prepare and refine radioactives, even withdrawing them from the depths of the planet."

"That," Abna said, looking at the Amazon and Viona, "sounds as though there might be a lot of radioactivity below surface. We'd better keep clear of anything below this level...."

Turning again, he surveyed the men and women workers who had now come forward to form a circle.

Their expressions were wondering and their interest plain.

"Take the guns from these guards," Abna ordered, and two of the workers promptly obeyed.

"How long will that neutralization machine stay in action?"

"As long as need be. I do not understand its principle but I have heard say it will operate indefinitely."

"Soon find out," the Amazon murmured, and with lithe strides she hurried down the workshop to the instrument and examined it carefully. When she came back she was smiling confidently.

"Probably keep going forever," she announced. "It is linked up to underground radioactive sources, and as long as they remain the instrument will keep functioning. As near as I can tell it is disseminating a wave that easily covers all this workshop area and a good way beyond it. Workers in neighboring workshops should also come somewhat under its influence."

Abna nodded and looked quickly at Ilosa. "How many other workshops are there on this planet, Ilosa?"

"About thirty," she answered, after thinking for a moment. "And each one is under the dominance of the Mizanu, as this one is."

"And do they each have a neutralizing machine, like this one here?"

Ilosa nodded promptly. "Bound to have. There is never any telling when it might be necessary to halt the hypnosis for some reason or other."

Abna considered for a moment.

"The situation, my friends, is this," he said. "You are kindly, normal people who, if left to yourselves, would live more or less happy lives on this world of yours and gradually build up a structure of social and scientific progress. However, because of the fantastic scientific activities of certain beings on your neighbor world, you have become slaves of a planetary brain and, though you have not known it whilst under hypnosis, you have been building the necessary machines and materials for an intended universal conquest...."

There was a murmur of disbelief from the astonished workers, which stilled as Abna raised his hand.

"We of Earth have only one purpose—to try and help the oppressed and scientifically backward with whatever knowledge we have at our command. The menace of a planet that is an entire brain in itself cannot be allowed to exist. Somehow—by a means which is not yet clear to us—we must destroy the Mizanu."

"Destroy an entire planet which is capable of thinking for itself?" Ilosa exclaimed. "Surely that is impossible? It will be able to anticipate your actions."

Abna smiled indulgently. "Your knowledge of science is almost nonexistent, Ilosa, therefore it would be pointless for me to try to explain how we shall begin the extermination, and I certainly would not give any details openly, since by means of radio-vision waves— if you know what that means—the Mizanu even now knows what I am saying and is also watching me. Reprisals, I fear, will soon be attempted."

There was silence, the workers completely attentive and more than willing to follow the leadership of this squat, immensely powerful man who with the two beautiful Earth-women had come into their drab, regimented existence.

"The first move," Abna said, "is to stage a revolution. That means a complete defiance of the Mizanu, and that defiance can be maintained as long as the neutralizers are used. Obviously, the first move the Mizanu will make will be to try and stop the source of power that feeds the neutralizers. Since that power is underground, you must delegate numbers amongst yourselves to keep constant watch. In that way only can you retain your own individualities and fight this battle which will soon be upon you."

"But surely, Earthman, you will lead us?" one of the workers asked.

"Our task lies in destroying the Mizanu itself," Abna replied. "You have your own individual initiatives and must learn to fight for yourselves. Your task must be to overpower the guards of the other workshops scattered throughout your planet and then set the neutralizers to work. Gather all you can to your banner and we of Earth will do the rest.... Now, our first move is to get out of this workshop."

"That," one of the guards remarked, as Abna jumped down from his high perch, "you will not find so simple, man of Earth. The only way out of here is by that opening there—and the steel slide has been closed across it."

"Then get it removed!" Abna commanded; and at

that the guards looked at one another and guffawed.

"The lock," one of them explained, "works on a combination principle, and you have killed the man who understood it."

Abna studied it carefully for a while and then gave a questioning-glance toward the Amazon and Viona.

"Steel, copper, and a mixture of something else," he said. "Exceptionally hard and proof against even our guns, I'm afraid."

Experimentally he tried his gun on the barrier, but it was a complete waste of time. Frowning, he put the weapon away again, and said. "The sooner we find our way back to our space machine and then head for the world of the Mizanu, the better...."

He paused. Viona and the Amazon looked about them; the workers tensed and visible fear sprang into their faces. At the same moment each one of them heard a curious faraway whining note—a thin, edgy scream apparently coming from a great distance. And with the seconds it became louder.

"It's a directed missile!" It was one of the guards who gave the cry. "The Mizanu has fired it! Reprisal for the revolution you Earth fools have started."

His fury and fear were such that he darted from amongst his disarmed colleagues and flung himself on Abna, battering at him frenziedly with his heavy fists. Abna jolted backwards for a moment and then seized the man's wrist and flung him helplessly several feet away.

In those few seconds the scream of the descending

missile, evidently directed to this one particular spot by radio control, became louder.... And louder still.

CHAPTER EIGHT
THE CAPTURE OF VIONA

Petrified, the workers waited. For that matter, so did Abna, the Amazon, and Viona. Every eye was fixed on the high metal roof of the workshop; every face showed that escape was considered hopeless—as indeed it was in the short time left before the missile landed.

The scream rose to deafening sound and then suddenly the roof was a whirling cascade of incandescent light as some unholy explosive blasted downwards. Rocks and metal girders came hurtling inwards and downwards, flung by the expansion of gases. The workshop rocked, became clouded with acrid fumes. Din roared inwards and machines and instruments toppled.

Flung flat on their faces, the Earth trio waited until the confusion began to subside. Then they moved slowly, twinging from the cuts and bruises inflicted by jagged splinters of metal and stone. Of the workshop itself, only three-quarters of it remained, and this three-quarters was a shambles.

"Bomb of some sort," Abna muttered, struggling to his feet. "Not quite a direct hit, though...."

The Amazon and Abna rose beside him. Their eyes traveled over the twisted, shattered figures of the scores of workers who had been obliterated—among them Ilosa, who lay quite near, crushed by fallen rock. Those who had survived were in the smoky distances, dazed, wandering stupidly around, and trying to get their bearings.

In spite of the ferocity of the attack, evidently intended as a reprisal blow for the plan of revolution, it had failed in its basic objective. For one thing, the three from Earth were still very much alive, and for another, the neutralizer, though covered in fine dust, was still in action.

"Any chance of a mind-over-matter resurrection for these people?" Viona asked quickly, glancing at her father.

He shook his head. "No time. An onslaught like this is proof positive that the Mizanu is moving fast to get this revolution under control. We've got to move even faster...."

"Funny the Mizanu missed the target," the Amazon commented, staring up the side of the mighty crater toward the evening light above. "Probably the missile was sent hastily and missed being dead on the target for that reason."

Abna was not listening. Realizing the need for quick action, he hurried forward and clambered on to the nearest dust-covered machine. The sound of his powerful voice stilled the wanderings of the survivors and they paused to listen to him.

"Everything I said before this attack was made still goes!" he cried. "You are pledged now to revolt against your oppressor and to bring the rest of your race to your side. You will run grave dangers in your endeavors—of which this is a sample—but that is only to be expected. Contact your comrades in the other workshops: see that their neutralizers are brought into action. Do everything you can— For my colleagues and I there is now a way of escape by means of the bomb crater; and we are taking it. Our objective is the neighbor world itself."

Abna hurried across to the sloping crater wall; Viona and the Amazon were already scrambling up it as hurriedly as the loose, still-warm ash would permit. As Abna crawled up the crater side, the Amazon and Viona were about two yards higher ahead of him. Suddenly Viona, the farthest up the slope, gave a cry of consternation.

Abna and the Amazon lifted their heads—and met the unpleasant sight of nearly 100 guards on the edge of the crater.

Evidently they had been dispatched hurriedly either from the neighbor world itself—which was unlikely in so short a time—or else from another region of Axilon. The only advantage at the moment seemed to be that they were half blinded by the intolerable glare of the low-lying suns. Shielding their eyes, they were peering into the crater's depths and talking among themselves.

"What do we do?" the Amazon asked, as Abna scrambled to her side. "Try picking them off?"

"Not that, Vi—too many of them." Then he called, "Viona! Come back here—"

Viona did not hear him: his voice was too low-pitched. She was still ascending the crater side, the glint of her gun visible in her hand. With all the reckless impetuosity of youth, retreat was the last thing that suggested itself to her.

"The little fool!" Abna breathed. "What does she think she can do against that mob?"

"Wipe them out, of course! I think the same! We can't leave her to tackle it alone, Abna."

"And throw our lives away as well? That isn't sense!"

The Amazon did not comment, but she moved her gun round and bent her head to sight it. Her intention of firing at the guards who still stood at the crater edge was not realized, for Abna's grip on her arm tightened—and it was the kind of grip that even her superhuman strength could not dislodge.

"What are you trying to do?" she demanded, her voice, hoarse with anger. "Let Viona go to her death?"

At that moment Viona, lying flat in the ashes close to the crater top, pressed the switch of her gun. With a scything motion she swept the disintegrative beam across the assembled men. They dropped like cornstalks before the reaper.

Not all of them were affected, and these survivors blasted forth with their own guns. Around Viona's sprawled form ash spouted and hazed under the energy generated by the heat guns. Viona, to whom fear was an unknown quantity, stayed where she was and fired back.

In a matter of seconds the guards came plunging down the slope, three more of their numbers tottering before Viona's gun in the process. The others reached her and, since they did not fire at her again, it seemed they had had orders not to kill her. She was hauled to her feet, her gun snatched from her, and in a matter of moments was surrounded.

"Nothing we can do with this," Abna said.

The Amazon began to protest, in as vehement a voice as she dared, but Abna disregarded her. Still holding onto her arm he forced her down the slope in a slithering run—but such a retreat could hardly be made in silence. There were cries from the guards above and half a dozen of them began to plunge downwards, knee-deep in ashes at every leap.

Gaining the workshop floor, dimly lighted now thanks to the partial failure of power, Abna looked quickly about him. One or two workers were still scattered around, apparently staying to guard what remained of the machines and the still operative neutralizer. The others had vanished, and the gaping manhole that led to the underworld seemed to be the answer.

"That's our next move," Abna decided abruptly. "Come...."

Realizing by now that it was inevitable that Viona must be abandoned, the Amazon streaked after him across the cracked and fissured flooring, reaching the manhole lip only a few seconds behind him. To the rear the guards had just completed their stumbling descent of the crater and were firing with blind ferocity. The beams missed the Amazon by some feet as she hastily scrambled down the metal ladder in Abna's wake.

Twenty feet below the Amazon found Abna waiting for her. Together they looked about them. In these depths there was lighting of sorts provided by strings of pale yellow lamps. Possibly their dimness was caused by the lowered power supply, but at least there was enough illumination to behold a tunnel, man-gouged out of solid rock, extending in both directions as far as the eye could see.

"Either way will do," Abna said, as there came the sound of the guards' hurrying feet above. "We'll take left."

They did, running with the speed and precision of trained athletes. Neither of them had the least idea where they were heading, of course; they could only blindly hope that somehow they would contact either the surface or a bunch of workers who could give them some geographical directions. At the moment these mine workings were completely deserted, probably because the workers who had already descended had taken everybody possible unto their banner in their flight to the next nearest workshop.

To the rear of the running two there presently came the distinct echoing footfalls of the pursuing guards. The Amazon glanced over her shoulder and then gave Abna a glance.

"We ought to settle with them, Abna, if only to make ourselves safe. They're going to hamper us all the time if we don't."

"Perhaps be a spot somewhere ahead where we can nab them," he responded quickly. "We certainly dare not stop in the middle of a straight tunnel like this; they'd get us instantly."

The unexpected happened before they were ready for it. A half-mile farther on the tunnel took a sharp right-angled turn and then suddenly ended at the clean-cut edge of a shaft. Around the shaft top were machines of various types, most of them electronic and obviously much used. Halfway round the rim of the shaft were rails of narrow gauge, and upon them half a dozen partly loaded trucks that had been abandoned. Again it looked like a case of workers having been snatched from their activities.

"We can't get round this!" the Amazon exclaimed, looking anxiously about her. "The walls close right in to this tunnel and the only way to get at those machines must be by means of yet another subterranean passageway."

"And we can't jump it either." Abna peered intently across the dark gap of the shaft, but so wide was it he could not descry the other side.

"What's in it, I wonder?" The Amazon peered over the edge and looked below. At an infinite depth she fancied she could see a dim glow—a curious phosphorescent haze.

"Probably a radioactive ocean or something," Abna said, gazing down with her. "Far enough down for us not to be affected by it.... I hope."

Then he looked up sharply. The sound of hurrying feet was again becoming evident, growing louder and chasing the echoes of this satanic region.

"Guards still after us!" The Amazon looked over her shoulder. "And no way forward either—"

"But there's enough room here," Abna interrupted her, pointing to a recess in which stood the machine which was nearest the shaft edge. "It will keep us out of sight to begin with. After that we'll have to deal with our annoying friends as prudence dictates."

He dived for the opening with the Amazon behind him. They had hardly squeezed themselves into the recess before the guards came round the corner of the short right-angled passage. It was the same six who had chased them all the way from the bomb crater. Now they came gradually to a halt, breathing hard, looking about them in the dim glow of the roof lights.

"Something strange here," one of the guards said, looking at his comrades. "They couldn't possibly have got across the shaft: they'd not have time to push the bridge into place and withdraw it. And to get around the shaft, they'd have to detour into the other corridor which would mean going back several miles."

"Maybe they can vanish into the air," another of the men suggested. "They're from another world, remember. Got strange powers, perhaps."

In the shadows of the recess the Amazon carefully eased her gun from her belt inside heir overalls. Then she leveled it—and this time Abna did not stop her. He had drawn his own gun also.

"Just a chance I can mow the lot of them down," the'
Amazon murmured. sighting carefully. "In case I slip
up, follow up my fire."

"Right." Abna raised his own gun and took aim.

But, by some unknown obstinacy, no disintegrating
beam jetted forth from the Amazon's gun when she
pressed the button. Instead there was a dull whirring—and that was all. She knew instantly what had
happened. The electrode contacts upon which the power
relied had locked themselves. It happened sometimes,
and there was no cure for it. It was just one of those
unknown factors which are present in almost all precision equipment— But the guards heard the whirring
and immediately twirled round, their own guns ready.
Abna fired, bringing two of the men down immediately before two more closed with him. The Amazon
for her part found herself overwhelmed, the remaining
two guards not choosing to use their heat beams upon
her. Instead they battered savagely at her head with the
butt ends of the heavy instruments, bringing her down
to her knees.

Her gun fell from her hand and was immediately
seized. Then another smashing blow across the back
of her neck flattened her on the edge of the shaft rim.
Abna lashed out savagely and flung one of his attackers
back into the tunnel. The remaining one he killed on
the spot with his gun, the awful power exploding the
guard into ashes and spattering water.

A heat beam flashed from one of the guards pinning
the Amazon. The searing fire cut straight across Abna's

arm and chest. Even his physique could not absorb the shock and he half collapsed, his weapon dropping from his numbed hand. It hit the stony floor and rolled to within a few inches of the Amazon's hand. She reached out towards it, then a boot heel crashed down on her fingers.

The impact of this shock together with the pain of it jolted the daze out of her brain. She realized she was pinned face down on the edge of the shaft, one man's weight holding down her legs, and the other kneeling on her shoulders.

Abruptly heaving upward with all her strength, using her hands and arms to spring her, she pitched one of the men from his perch. He reeled helplessly into the void and then hurtled down the shaft, his dying scream echoing back until it was lost amidst a sullen splashing.

The remaining guard presented no difficulty as far as the Amazon was concerned. Abna, she saw, was out of the fight for the moment. He was sitting crouched, hand holding his damaged arm, his face a mask of concentration. Plainly he was struggling to exert the superb strength of his mind over the material condition and restore himself to normal—but that, with intense pain overpowering him, might take time.

CHAPTER NINE
THE RADIUM OCEAN

The Amazon closed with the guard who had been pinning her legs. He made one hopeless effort to use his gun. Failing, he sought to overpower what appeared to be a slim woman in overalls. And in this he made the same mistake as many an enemy before him. Once within the steel grip of the Golden Amazon there was no way of escape. Fingers of fiendish power cracked the bones in his wrist. Muscles of pile-driver force impelled a fist straight into his face. The impact was so violent he was dead from shock even as he was lifted from the ground—then he was flying outwards into the center of the shaft...and dropped.

Only just in time the Amazon spun round as the one remaining guard dived for her. He had been flung back into the tunnel by Abna, but by this time had recovered. With an adroit backward leap the Amazon missed his bull rush and at the same time delivered a pole-axing blow with her sound fist to the back of his neck.

He grunted, crumpled, and clawed at emptiness.... Then he, too, was far out over the shaft and vanished into its depths. Only that faint splashing disturbed the echoes when a few seconds had passed.

Slowly the Amazon straightened, breathing hard and peering at her bleeding fingers in the dim light. She moved across to where Abna was slowly standing up, all signs of injury upon his arm and chest now having disappeared. He gave a taut smile.

"Bit difficult," he said quietly. "That heat beam stopped my heart. However...."

The Amazon stared at him. "You mean you stayed conscious with your heart stopped? But that amounts to defeating death!"

"Well?" Abna raised his eyebrows. "What of it? I defeated it once before, remember, on Jupiter. When we first met. Death doesn't really exist, Vi: it's nothing more than a very strong illusion. But that's enough of that: what's wrong with your hand?"

"Badly crushed." The Amazon held it out, her mouth taut.

Abna smiled and held the broken, bleeding fingers gently for a while. He even went to the length of putting his free arm around the Amazon's supple shoulders and holding her against him.

Nor did she seem to resent it as she usually did—unless she was glad of his ministrations with anguish biting at her. She only began to stir fretfully as the pain subsided and she withdrew her hand to find it as perfect as it had been before.

"Funny stuff, physical matter," Abna reflected. "Does just as you tell it when you use sufficient mental control. And so it should! It's only one of the grosser states anyhow, whereas mind is the highest state of all."

Surprisingly, he delivered a kiss on the Amazon's mouth as she stood looking at him.

"We'd better decide what to do next," the Amazon said.

"Find a way to the surface, naturally. We could go back the way we've come, I suppose?"

"We could, but we'd probably encounter more guards. What we have to do is to try and rescue Viona; or failing that, get to the *Ultra* and head for the neighbor-world. Maybe we can strike a bargain with the Mizanu; and if that doesn't work we'll perhaps think up a way to destroy him."

"You seem," the Amazon said, "to be assuming that all is well with Viona. By this time she's probably dead."

"I don't think she will be. I haven't forgotten how these guards went to great pains not to injure her. My guess is that she's needed alive, probably for examination by the Mizanu. We are of an alien world, remember, and therefore of special interest. Come to think of it, those guards didn't try to kill us, either. Their efforts were confined to wounding or overpowering us."

"And you with your heart stopped by a heat ray? What was that? Just getting playful?"

"Wasn't intentional, I don't think. I just happened to catch the beam at that point...." Abna moved to the shaft edge. "That guard said something about a bridge to cross this. Wonder what he meant?"

He found out in a moment or two as his investigating

fingers pressed a switch set in the edge of the shaft. Instantly a bridge ejected itself from a concealed slot and shot, quivering, across the abyss, much as a spring rule might shoot from its spool.

"Very nice," Abna commented, studying it. "Our weight upon it will cause it to gently bend down so we reach the other side comfortably. At least, I suppose so: from here I can't even see where the bridge finishes. Anyway, ready to risk it?"

The Amazon nodded and followed Abna as he set foot on the bridge. Then with perfect poise he began walking along its narrow length. Below there was nothing but the shaft's yawning void with the dim mysterious glow far in the depths.

"This shaft is over 1,000 feet deep," the Amazon said at length, when they were far enough across the bridge to be unable to see either side of the shaft anymore.

"How do you know?"

"I estimated it from the time one of the guards took to fall to the moment of the splash...."

Abna did not say anything. He was feeling his way carefully now with his feet, still having sufficient mastery over himself not to need to go on all fours. The Amazon kept her hand on the belt of his tunic and moved when he did.

"This shaft must be an enormous distance across," he said after a while. "We've been going quite a while and there's no sign of lights from the other side."

"Maybe because they're countersunk into the ceiling, or rather roof. That hides the direct rays from us. I noticed how quickly the lights to rearward faded as we moved out over the shaft. Incidentally, this spring bridge is a clever idea. I suppose a button on the ether side starts an electric current which causes the bridge to roll back into its former place?"

"S'pose so." Abna kept on going steadily, and the darkness was appalling, though not quite so much so as that mysterious glowing enigma in the far-flung depths.

It was after five more minutes of careful forward advance that Abna suddenly paused, feeling at something that had come into his carefully outstretched hand. It was something very solid and very cold, apparently oval in shape and hanging in mid-air.

"It's a huge chain of some kind," the Amazon said, investigating with him. "A link, nearly two feet long. Must be something on the end of it."

"Naturally," Abna's dry voice conceded. "Probably some kind of dredging apparatus operated from a point a little way above us."

Then as he did not move on the Amazon said:

"What's the matter? Something occurred to you?"

"Yes. I was just thinking that if we climbed down this chain, we might be able to see at close quarters what that luminous stuff is below. It fascinates me. It may be something worth recording in our scientific annals."

"I'm more interested in finding Viona or the *Ultra*."

"So am I, but this is a chance not to be missed. With links of this size there'll be no more difficulty than descending a ladder."

She followed him as he grasped the giant link and then, began to lower himself into the depths.

"It's unbelievable," Abna said presently, awe in his voice, and the Amazon looked at him. With the reflection of light from the ocean and the accustomedness of her eyes to the darkness she could discern his expression fairly clearly. He looked astonished beyond measure.

"Certainly an extraordinary sight," the Amazon agreed. "It reminds me of nothing so much as blue milk about to boil—"

"This stuff," Abna interrupted, "is an ocean having seventy-five percent radium content. Incredible, staggering wealth—as judged from Earth standards. Here, take a look at this detector of mine."

The Amazon did so and there was no gainsaying that steadily pointing needle on the "75" mark. When she came to consider the fabulous value of even a gram of radium back on Earth, she began to realize Abna's amazement. In this luminous ocean there was radium untold—and with it deadly radioactivity.

"We'd better get out," she said.

Abna seemed in no hurry. "Presumably this crucible is used to haul the stuff up to the surface, after which it is perhaps refined in some way or other, as on Earth we refine crude oil. All of it necessary to keep the Mizanu in existence.... We've seen many things in our travels, Vi, but a radium ocean is a new one."

"Not all ocean either," she said, after a moment.

"Look down there to the left. It's black with luminous wavelets rippling against it. Looks like ground of some sort."

Feeling inside her uniform she pulled a small food container from her belt and tossed it downward. Almost instantly there was a clinking sound as the container, struck something solid instead of being absorbed into the deadly ocean.

"Definitely hard ground—probably rock," Abna said, and there was something about his tone that left the sentence unfinished.

"You're thinking we should explore down there, aren't you?" the Amazon questioned presently.

"Why not? We've come down this far—"

"But what about the radioactivity? We're getting more impregnated every moment."

"Can't you rely on me to put our physical difficulties right? We'll probably find a way out to the surface this way."

Abna hauled himself up to the lip of the crucible, scrambled over the edge and then let himself drop. He fell no more than twelve feet and landed on the solid area without harm. After a moment or two the Amazon dropped beside him, and together they stood on this weirdly dark 'shore' staring at the incoming wavelets of gleaming light.

"This a tidal ocean, do you think?" the Amazon asked. "If it is, we may get caught up in it."

Abna was silent for a while, watching the wavelets; then:

"The stuff isn't coming any nearer. No tide to worry about. Let's get on the move...." With every step they took they could feel an increase in the intolerable smarting of their exposed skin. The Amazon was just about to mention it when she realized that the discomfort had ceased.

"Better?" Abna asked.

"Your mind-over-matter act again, I suppose?"

"Naturally. I don't see why we should be dictated to by our bodies when we've important investigation to make. Whatever radioactivity there is won't harm us from here on."

Nor did it. They both felt perfectly normal as they continued their advance, even though it occurred to the Amazon once or twice that without Abna's amazing metaphysical powers they would by now probably be dying of burns from the inexorable power of free gamma radiations.

"Has it occurred to you yet what we are walking on?" Abna asked finally, and at that the Amazon stopped and kicked the rock at her feet experimentally. She noticed something now that she had not noticed before, however. The plateau was not nearly so hard as it had at first seemed. Indeed, the toe of her heavy shoe left a faintly gleaming dent in the ground.

"Lead!" she exclaimed, going down on one knee and looking more closely.

"Correct! A plateau of lead—and there isn't anything very surprising about that, since radium finally mutates into lead. At one time I suppose that ocean reached this far."

They went on again, to find that the shore presently began to narrow sharply, forcing them to move inward until they were close beside the cavern wall. Gazing intently ahead of them in the weird light they could faintly see an acclivity reaching upward into the profound darkness.

"Good!" Abna exclaimed. "With a bit of luck we'll find our way to the surface even yet, and without the distraction of guards, too."

Before long they reached the rough upward path and found that it climbed at a sharp angle, so much so they had to clamber here and there over lead boulders to find the acclivity's continuation. It was when they felt they had ascended about half the distance of the shaft that Abna called a halt.

"Time we relaxed and had something to eat. We can't go on forever without nourishment."

The Amazon murmured an assent and settled down amidst the rocks. In the interest of the exploration she had overlooked the fact that she was ravenously hungry: now she came to dwell upon it, it insisted on being noticed.

Each of them withdrew several small containers from their belts beneath their overalls and in silence partook of a concentrated meal, finishing it off with liquid pastilles that provided a copious, restorative drink.

"This is a truly amazing System," Abna remarked at last. "The first one we've come across which is highly radioactive."

"With Nur as the most radioactive of all. It surprises me that these slave people of Axilon don't suffer more from the radioactive emanations which must constantly be around them."

"To a certain extent they seem physically inured," Abna responded. "But of course a direct contact with radioactives produces devastating effects, as in the case of that woman in the workshop who got so badly burned—" Abna broke off, looking intently at the dark wall of the cavern beside him. "Take a look at that, Vi! Copper! Vein after vein of it!"

The Amazon nodded. "I noticed it as we came up the acclivity." She snapped her fingers: "Abna, what fools we are! Both of us with wrist-television—and Viona possessing one too—and we've made no attempt to see if we can contact her."

"Seems to me there hasn't been much chance until now," Abna responded, holding forth his wrist and adjusting the highly-sensitive, watch-sized equipment with the tiny circular screen.

Here in the deep bluish gloom both his instrument and the Amazon's were clearly visible as far as the screens were concerned, and they both tensed forward as, instead of the blank they had expected, there merged into view what appeared to be some kind of office—or, more accurately, a guardroom. Viona herself was not visible, which was not surprising since the instrument making this transmission would be on her wrist, but there was a lopsided picture of a harsh-faced guard seated at a desk, and he appeared to be looking straight into the screen. Evidently Viona was standing facing him, but whether she was alone or not was not clear. The tilted effect of the view was caused by her arm being at her side, with the wrist-transmitter-receiver at right angles to the scene.

"Good for Viona," Abna murmured, studying the picture intently. "Never misses a trick. She's switched the thing on so we can pick up the scene if at all possible, even though she herself is not able to speak at the moment."

CHAPTER TEN
BANISHMENT

The guard was saying: "...and all of you should have had more sense than to allow yourselves to be duped by this woman of Earth and her two colleagues. You should have realized that a revolution could not succeed."

"So the revolution has been obliterated," Abna murmured. "That's not pleasant hearing, Vi, after all our efforts."

"Couldn't expect much else with a lot of unscientific, browbeaten people handling things. We should have stayed and directed them. I expect they played clean into the guards' hands—"

"For those who defy the Mizanu or attempt to overthrow his domination, there is one fixed, unvarying punishment," the head guard resumed abruptly. "That punishment is banishment to Nur, there to die...."

Sounds of protest and fury floated through the minute speaker at which the guard slammed his big hand down on the desk.

"Silence! You have heard the sentence, and within one hour it will be carried out.... Take them out!"

The view swung and lurched as Viona was evidently seized and forced out of the guardroom. There followed a 'tumbled backward' view of a corridor, then the Amazon snapped off her instrument and jumped to her feet.

"On our way, quick!" she snapped, then she hesitated again as Abna only rose leisurely to his feet, snapping off his own wrist-televisor as he did so.

"No matter how quickly we try and go, we can't possibly reach her in time," he said quietly.

"We can try, can't we? Why don't you get to grips with the situation; Abna? Viona's going to be sent to that hell-world, that radioactive planet of Nur, and that means she'll die—and horribly. How you can stand there and calmly say we—"

"I'm speaking truth, and you know it."

The Amazon still hesitated, then her eyes brightened under a sudden thought

"What about instantaneous transportation? We've done it before in an emergency—or at least you've done it for yourself, Viona, and me. We could instantly transmit ourselves mentally to where Viona is and rescue her."

"I'd thought of that. The difficulty is that we don't know where she is, so that rules out thought-transportation. In any case I doubt if I'd be up to a successful thought-transportation. I've been doing a lot of hard mental work to defeat the effects of radioactivity and I'm somewhat fatigued."

The Amazon looked annoyed, then she swung away

and started to continue the journey up the acclivity. After a while Abna caught up with her.

"No use your getting all steamed up with me, Vi. This is one case where mental power isn't much use. We obviously can't project ourselves to an unknown destination and trust to luck; anything could happen. The only possible move we can make is get to the surface, find the *Ultra*, and then get to Nur in time—if we can—to snatch Viona before the radioactivity of that planet kills her."

"Yes," the Amazon muttered, climbing upwards vigorously. "I suppose that is the only way.... If only she were as well versed in metaphysics as you, Abna! You've taught her what to do, but she won't concentrate. Now she needs metaphysical knowledge to save her life."

"The young dislike to concentrate," Abna sighed. "Can't blame the girl for that. Apparently the only way to free the slaves of Axilon is to destroy the power that dominates them. They just haven't the initiative to start a revolution of their own."

With that their conversation ceased. Both of them had the inner conviction that if only they could reach the surface in time, and be favored then by a slice of luck, they could still find Viona and save her before the dread banishment to Nur.... Both of them remembered too their vision of that ghastly world, glowing with its luminous internal fires. Any ruling authority, however dominant, sending flesh-and-blood captives to such a planet must be utterly devoid of all sentiment—and for that reason if none other, the satanic power of the Mizanu must be destroyed—and quickly.

* * * * * * *

The upwardly climbing two were thankful to discover that nothing impeded them, even though here and there they had to almost become mountaineers to overcome some of the tougher parts of the acclivity. Thus they came finally to the upper levels and found they had emerged through a natural blowhole in the rocks, and were standing beneath the stars in the midst of a cool night breeze. At least it felt cool after the underworld and their memory of the torrid day.

"Night on Axilon," Abna murmured, gazing around him. "Very interesting! Take a look at those stars, Vi! Utterly different from anything seen from Earth—the whole swirling mass of the First Galaxy right on top of us as it were.... Yes, and see there! The diamond bright star low down on the horizon! That's our own sun, I do believe!"

"No doubt of it," the Amazon admitted at length. "I don't suppose we'd see as small a sun as ours at this distance were it not for the clearness of this atmosphere...." She gazed overhead at the awesome sight of the incredibly near Milky Way and the spawning island universes beyond it; then her fantastic appreciation of the celestial deeps was suddenly overcome by the remembrance of more immediate things.

"We've no time to waste looking at the stars!" she exclaimed. "We've got to find Viona! Whereabouts are we, do you think?"

"No idea, but I can soon discover. Certainly we're a. long way from any of the workers' cities. Not one in sight anywhere."

As he spoke Abna withdrew from the belt inside his overalls the compass that was automatically tuned upon the *Ultra*. It operated by the needle being magnetically drawn towards the *Ultra*'s atomic power plant and, as usual, it was completely unerring. It swung back and forth for a second or two and then came to rest, pointing diagonally ahead.

"Seven or eight miles," Abna announced. "Let's get moving."

They wasted no more time. Hurrying over the drab terrain of Axilon, they nonetheless kept their attention alert for any signs of attack. Not that they expected any, having emerged so far from one of the workers' cities—but if danger did come they would have only their wits and muscles to rely upon, their guns being lost. For the moment the starry darkness was their friend, cloaking their rapid advance.

They had about completed half their journey when they suddenly paused as a rumbling roar smote upon their ears. From long accustomedness they instantly analyzed it as the take-off discharge of a rocket-projectile, a belief that was confirmed a moment later as, some miles away, a blazing javelin streaked into the night sky, shattering the echoes with its ever-rising scream. Silent, faces upturned, Abna and the Amazon watched until the fiery cascade was swallowed up amongst the stars—then they looked at each other.

"Probably the prison ship," Abna muttered. 'Unfortunately, both Nur and the neighbor world are hidden from us at the moment, being in the opposite hemisphere of Axilon, otherwise we'd have had some idea of the projectile's direction.... I'm afraid we're too late to save Viona."

"Then we'll head to Nur the moment we reach the *Ultra*," the Amazon decided, and increased her swift walking into a run—and kept it up. So finally the *Ultra* came into view and, behind it, loomed the city of the workers where their adventures had commenced.

Once within the control room, the Amazon shut the airlock quickly whilst Abna turned to the power plant in readiness to load it up. Then he gave a gasp of consternation.

"What?" The Amazon's face was anxious as she came to his side.

"Empty!" He gave her a grim look. "Matrix denuded of copper—and there was a little left—and the spares have all gone too! This is the work of those guards! They know, or have been told by the Mizanu, that copper is our motive power; so they've grounded us."

"Only one thing for it," the Amazon decided, and tugging off her hampering overalls she then crossed to the weapon-rack and took down a fully charged disintegrator gun. "We've got to go back below and grab some of that copper we saw. Get yourself a gun while I fetch the rock-cutting equipment."

Abna nodded quickly, but he did not immediately

take a gun from the weapon-rack. Instead he crossed to the electronic-controller in a further corner of the chamber and switched it on. In a matter of moments he had been restored to his normal seven feet of height, and with a rueful grin he clambered out of the overalls that had now burst apart with his increase in size.

"Abna, we're in a hurry!" the Amazon told him impatiently, as she returned with the rock-cutter slung over her shoulder. "What does it signify whether you're normal height or not?"

"Signifies a great deal—to me. You've no idea how difficult it is to accustom yourself to lesser size. Strides, reach, and everything else are all wrong. No point in trying to look like a worker anymore, so I may as well be natural.... Got everything?"

"Everything! Let's be moving."

There was a sudden sharp command from the darkness ahead. Dim figures appeared, barring the path.

"Halt and identify yourselves, otherwise we fire!"

The Amazon set her mouth harshly and raised her gun; then Abna put his hand on her arm.

"Wait a moment! Those don't look like guards. From their untidy silhouettes I'd say they're workers in overalls—" He raised his voice, "I am Abna of Earth. With me is my woman colleague, the Amazon of Earth."

"You lie! Abna of Earth is a smallish, broad man. You are a giant! Declare yourselves afresh...."

"I have declared the truth!" Abna snapped. "My size is merely a matter of electronic control. You are workers, the ones we tried to help. Do you recall the

incident when I cured the two on the workshop floor—
the woman who had radioactive burns and the man
whom the guard blasted with his gun?"

CHAPTER ELEVEN
MAROONED ON NUR

"Yes, they are the Earth people," one of them muttered. Then in a louder voice he added: "We thought you dead."

"We're obviously alive and full of regret that the revolution against Mizanu failed—"

"The revolution did not fail!" the worker snapped. "How else would we be free of the city, free of hypnosis, and on the watch for guards who might try to overthrow us?"

At that the tension broke. The guards moved forward, feeling quickly at the Amazon and Abna with friendly hands, as though to make sure they were indeed alive.

"I don't understand this," Abna said finally. "Our woman friend Viona was captured and through her, by means of television—which you will not understand—we heard a head guard say the revolution had been crushed. You say otherwise?"

"It is not yet planet-wide, but it certainly succeeded in the area where it began. We followed your orders and contacted other workshops. Now half the workers of Axilon are free of domination and the guards are in confusion. The neutralizers are springing into action everywhere, which accounts for our immunity from the Mizanu's hypnosis.... The head guard was lying and obviously speaking from headquarters where revolution has not yet struck. We too saw the prison projectile taking off."

"And we're getting after it!" the Amazon declared. "But we have to get copper first from the underworld."

"Copper? That reddish-gold substance?"

"That's it." Abna confirmed. "The sooner the better."

"You shall have a full escort to protect you from possible sneak attacks by guards," the worker declared. "Come with us."

Then as Abna and the Amazon followed him quickly in the direction of the city, he added. "We have to be very careful. The guards are still numerous and they are not trying to strike at us only because they know we outnumber them. Their aim is to stop the neutralizers from working and thereby allow the domination of the Mizanu to return. If that should happen, all we've fought for will be lost."

"Not necessarily," the Amazon said. "A thought just occurs to me. Down at the lowest depths of the underworld there is an ocean of radium and, skirting it, a plateau of solid lead. Do you know of it?"

"The underground workers will; I do not. What point are you trying to make, Amazon of Earth?"

"Just this. Lead is a perfect insulator against thought waves or any other form of radiation, a fact of which you unscientific people will not be aware. You can still make yourselves safe if the neutralizers are put out of action by wearing lead helmets. And to make them does not require any scientific skill: they can be hammered into shape, since lead is a soft, ductile metal."

"Your knowledge," the worker said in admiration, "is something that amazes us all."

"But a word of warning," the Amazon added, as they hurried along. "That radium ocean gives forth dangerous burning rays which will kill any workers at close quarters. They must wear insulated suits—or don't you know what I mean by that?"

"Yes, I know. Some workers wear them, especially those who have below surface tasks to perform. I will see to it, Amazon, that your suggestion is carried out— and in safety. The areas to which you refer contains enough lead to supply helmets for every man, woman, and child on Axilon. It will help the revolution immeasurably and make us independent of the neutralizers."

The Amazon nodded and said no more on the subject.

Abna said: "There is no need for us to make the underworld descent at all. These workers know the underground even better than we do."

* * * * * * *

While her parents waited for their precious copper, Viona lay in the lowest depths of the prison projectile, chained with her colleagues to the metal wall. Most of them were only recovering consciousness after the takeoff. Viona herself, used to the frightful strain of acceleration and superhumanly strong in the bargain, had not been affected. Through the small porthole on a level with her eyes, she had watched Axilon fall away into the void until now it was a vast globe some 25,000 miles distant. Ahead lay the neighbor-world, the planetary brain, and behind it the balefully glowing orb of Nur—their destination.

"Woman of Earth, do you know anything of Nur?" her colleague asked presently—a slim, serious-faced woman worker with deadly fear in her eyes.

"Very little," Viona replied quietly.

"I have heard many stories about it. It is a planet that corrodes and destroys metal, stone, and flesh. How it can do that I cannot imagine. Perhaps the stories that are told of it are untrue. We have only the word of the guards, and they will only say what the Mizanu commands them to say."

"Unfortunately, I think they have spoken truth." Viona gave her a serious glance. "Nur is a world of what is called radioactivity, and you should know from the burns received by your own workers in the underground what that can do."

"Has radioactivity anything to do with gamma rays?"

"Everything." Viona looked surprised at such a question from one so unversed in science. "Why?"

"Because the only time when the Mizanu's grip is not so strong upon us is when gamma rays are very strongly in action, either from Nur or our double-sun. I overheard that from two of the guards one day when hypnosis was at the minimum."

"I see." Viona frowned for a moment, then spoke half to herself. "Presumably the Mizanu, being a planetary brain, will be extremely susceptible to gamma rays. That's an interesting point, even though it does not do us much good."

"I suppose," the woman said, after a while, "that it is the insulation of this projectile which keeps my colleagues and myself free of hypnosis? Indeed, it must be, because there's no neutralizer on board."

Viona nodded absently but did not say anything. Her agile mind was still toying with the gamma ray theory that her companion had so casually mentioned. Then Viona sighed. Where was the use of pursuing any theory to its conclusion when certain death was ahead? She was not fool enough to think that even her immense physical resistance could hold out indefinitely against a world corroding with atomic emanations. Within an hour—or less—of reaching the hell planet she would be dead, and as far as she knew there was not the least chance of rescue. Nor was there anything that could be done with her wrist-radio-television. Its range had definite limits, and 25,000 miles was an impossible distance over which to communicate.

So the slow, inexorable journey continued, and in the process the prison-projectile passed close by the neighbor-world of the Mizanu. Viona looked down upon it with renewed interest, knowing as she did now, that it was a planetary brain, but from this vantage point in space there was nothing to reveal it as being different from any other planet, unless it was that the general grayness of the landscape was actually nothing more than a vast network of nerve fiber!

Then at length the vessel began to slow down. Viona looked anxiously through the porthole, her colleague beside her. There was nothing to be seen outside except the sparkling grayness. Even the landscape was hidden in the atomic vapors.... Then the metal door of the prison-hold rattled and one of the guards came in, his sadistic face grinning in ugly triumph.

"We're a thousand feet above Nur's surface," he announced, "and that means the end of the journey for the lot of you. Get moving! We're not wasting any more time than we can help in this place!" He unfastened the chains and then stood back.

His gun motioned so there was nothing to do but to obey. With the stricken look of doom on their faces, captives from Axilon began to walk slowly to the doorway and passed beyond it into the narrow metal corridor. Viona hesitated momentarily as she passed the guard, wondering if perhaps something could be gained by a lightning attack. Though she was perfectly sure of her physical ability to gain the mastery, she nonetheless shelved the idea. The vessel must be crawling with guards and they would soon make short work of her. No, better to take everything passively and hope somehow that she would survive even when stranded on the hell-planet's surface.

Around a trapdoor in the corridor the guard ordered a halt.

"Against the wall there you'll see a dozen parachutes.

Get them strapped on."

* * * * * * *

The Amazon said: "We'll be too late to rescue Viona. You know as well as I do the devastating power of radioactivity, and I'm afraid Viona is too undisciplined to be able to nail herself down to metaphysical control."

"I know," Abna muttered. "Have to hope for the best, Vi, that's all. After all, we've only ourselves to blame. We could quite easily have led a life of comfortable retirement on Earth, but instead we chose to fling ourselves across twenty thousand billion miles of space to encounter this! We can hardly talk about Viona being undisciplined after that!"

The Amazon did not answer for a moment. Standing beside the port, she gazed out upon the eternal wastes of space, her attention mainly centered on the gray enigma that was the planetary brain. Her fists clenched suddenly, and she beat them gently on the ledge as the *Ultra* fled onward through the depths.

Alma glanced through the porthole and at length detected a bright speck in distant infinity. He gave a shrug as he glanced back toward the Amazon.

"See that? It means that the prisoners, including Viona, have been duly left on Nur, and some time ago too judging by the distance that vessel has covered on its return trip."

The Amazon came across from the telescope and through the porthole watched the slowly growing speck intently. The nearer it came, the more her smoldering violet eyes brightened.

"Here is our chance for the first reprisal," she breathed. "Once let that machine come within radius of our weapons and it will cease to exist! One blow and it will be dust!"

Abna sighed. "Pointless expenditure of power, don't you think?"

"For heaven's sake, Abna, what kind of a man are you?" the Amazon blazed at him. "Doesn't it mean anything to you that those fiends on that ship took Viona and the others to Nur and left them there?"

"Maybe they did, but they're merely following out orders. We need to destroy the guiding brain, not the minions."

"That may be your point of view, but it isn't mine! I've had reason before to reproach you for your almost nauseating sentimentality sometimes—and this is another example of it."

CHAPTER TWELVE
VENGEANCE OF THE AMAZON

The Amazon's eternal streak of ruthlessness and her vicious desire to exact vengeance now the chance was within her grasp had to be appeased. In any case there would probably be attack from them; they could hardly be expected to let the *Ultra* pass them without putting up some kind of show. Unless, there being no other spaceships in the system except those controlled by the Mizanu, the vessels carried no armaments. If so, then the Mizanu spaceship would be a sitting target.

"Suppose," came Abna's voice, as the Amazon at last got the vessel in the sights of the ejector, "there was some last-minute hitch and the prisoners were not dumped on Nur after all? If that did arise, Viona will be aboard that vessel!"

"She isn't," the Amazon retorted. "That machine is near enough now to be within range of wrist-television if Viona were upon it. I've just had a look at mine and there's no signal. She isn't there...and don't keep trying to put me off!"

Abna did not say any more.

"Now are you satisfied?" the Amazon demanded.

"They're firing at us with some primitive kind of high-velocity shell. No doubt they'd pierce ordinary armor, but not the super-tough hide of the *Ultra*! Now I wonder how they'll like this in return?"

Smiling bitterly to herself she pressed the ejector's button. Instantly there flashed from its snout on the outside of the vessel a super-x-hydrogen shell. Moving swiftly in free space, it was impossible to follow its flight. Its moment of impingement upon the Mizanu vessel, however, was more than obvious. There was a blinding flash of flame, brighter for a second than huge Alpha himself. After which the flame turned to searing orange, devouring everything within its radius.

The ship, large though it was, ceased to be. It dripped into molten metal, and this too was vaporized into dust under the dreadful heat. The *Ultra* rocked slightly in its hurtling rush as it crossed the scene of destruction; then the drifting dust which had been a vessel was left behind, a gray powder on the face of infinity.

Abna checked the course calmly and then said, "You'd better get your brain to work to decide how a whole planet is going to be destroyed at one blow. Quite frankly, I don't know the answer...."

Flying with its uninterrupted high velocity—even though the speed nowhere approached the awe-inspiring maximum achieved on the journey from Earth to Alpha Centauri—the *Ultra* came within range of gray, inscrutable Nur some three hours later. In silence the Amazon and Abna looked down upon it, its whirling, deadly clouds illumined by the glare of the double sun.

"A cauldron of death if ever there was one," the Amazon muttered. "Do you notice a curious scintillation in those clouds, Abna? It's an amazing thought, but I do believe it's caused by radioactivity. If so, heaven help Viona."

"Check up on it while I reduce speed," Abna said, busy with the controls.

The Amazon turned to the analyzing equipment and after a while gave forth her pronouncements. Her voice was unusually subdued.

"To call Nur a hell-planet is an understatement," she said, returning to the porthole and gazing through it.

'The instruments show a seventy-five percent output of gamma lays, the full 100 percent made up with alpha, beta, x-ray, and others which don't fall into our scientific knowledge. That planet is nothing more than a titanic ferment of radioactivity. It's a wonder it exists as a planet at all; one would almost expect it to be a core of sheer energy."

"In time it will become so," Abna said.

"We might go on searching forever in this stuff," the Amazon said hopelessly. "We can't even see the ground. How about making a landing and risking a trip outside? I'm prepared to take that chance."

"So am I, but I can't see what good it would do. We don't know the exact spot where Viona is—granting she's alive—and the coincidence of us happening upon her is just too much to expect."

The Amazon was silent for a moment, gazing onto

the incredible scene outside; then as a sudden thought struck her she looked at her wrist television. Nothing. It was blank, except for an occasional miniature explosion of sparks as radioactive waves affected it. Even if by some miracle Viona could be alive and transmitting, the outside conditions would have obliterated it.

"There's one way around this problem—and one only," Abna said finally, after another fifteen minutes of blind flying through the murk. "I'm going to try and contact her mind. I did it once when she was lost in the Fifth Plane of Matter, if you remember, so I can do it again. That is, if she is alive. If she is dead, then she's beyond recall. Here, take over the controls whilst I see what I can do."

The Amazon obeyed silently, handling the switches and panels with the assurance of long practice. Meanwhile she gave occasional glances at Abna as he sat on the nearby wall-bunk, his head in his hands, his whole bearing one of rigid concentration. Inwardly the Amazon admired his supreme metaphysical gifts, powers that had in time past enabled him to create an entire city by the force of mental conception alone. Outwardly she resented his ability to accomplish something that was beyond her. Possibly she would never reach his metaphysical powers, because she was of Earth and he of Jupiter, which meant that they were each gifted along different lines.

Ten minutes passed, then Abna suddenly looked up sharply, his handsome face drawn with strain, yet his blue eyes intent and eager.

"At least she's alive! I can sense that!"

"She is? Oh, thank heaven!"

"Far as I can determine, she is also conscious. Even if she were unconscious I'd still be able to contact her because thought never ceases. Not even after death. But the trouble with after-death contact is that you're ruled by a mental image of the living body and with that being extinct, it upsets your calculations and—"

"Never mind that!" The Amazon's voice was impatient. "Where is she? Can we get to her?"

"At the moment she's a long way off; her vibrations are so faint I can hardly detect them. Keep on the present course and we'll see if we're going toward her or away from her."

"Are you still in touch with her?" the Amazon asked anxiously after a few minutes, and Abna nodded.

"Definitely. She's only a few yards from this spot, but I don't know in which direction. You'd better stay here while I go and investigate."

The Amazon brought the *Ultra* down to the surface. Then she hesitated as he turned toward the airlock. He gave a slow smile.

"Don't worry about me, Vi. I'm well able to take care of myself. The only way to find Viona is to search. And here I go.... You'd better seal yourself in the pressure chamber for a moment whilst I open and shut this airlock. I'm not sure how deadly the atmosphere might be."

Reluctantly, the Amazon turned away to the door of the nearby pressure-chamber, opened it, and then stepped beyond. Abna waited until the pressure-chamber door had closed again, and then he opened the big airlock.

Instantly, there came upon him that unbearable tingling and itching that had afflicted Viona. He disregarded it, stepped outside, and closed the airlock after him by means of the external screws.

Immediately he was amid the conditions which Viona had had experienced before him, but whereas she had found them increasingly too much for her, he stood for awhile weighing up the situation and at the same time exerting his mental control to prevent his body being overwhelmed. In five minutes he was master of the situation, and the unbearable burning sensation ceased. He began to move, and then caught sight of the Amazon's head and shoulders framed in the main outlook port as she watched him intently.

He smiled and waved in the searchlight glare, then went on into the murk. Within the *Ultra* the Amazon settled herself to wait, gazing after Abna until at last his immensely tall, powerful figure vanished in the drifting wreaths.

Here he felt entirely alone. The searchlight's radiance had completely faded—as though it had never been—so dense was the intervening radioactive fog. Abna also realized that there would be the difficulty of finding his way back to the *Ultra*, for the compass that normally pointed the way was as useless as all other instruments on this mad world. His only chance was to find Viona quickly. If he did not, he must return to the *Ultra* whilst he still knew its direction, and fasten a steel thread to it whilst he played it out after him in going farther afield.

CHAPTER THIRTEEN
THE SAVING OF VIONA

As he advanced he called Viona by name, but no answer was forthcoming. Ever and again he stopped and concentrated, until he once more picked up her mental vibrations. They told him an unmistakable story of anguish, even a conviction of near-death. He had to hurry if he were not to be too late.

The darkness hampered him. In this he did not have the advantage of the murky gloom that passed for daylight, for Nur had now turned on its axis and the night had come—dark, deadly night shot through with the eternal iridescent sparkle of electrical interchange.

Then, unexpectedly, Abna's search ended, but it probably would not have done so had his attention not been suddenly caught by something glowing on the leaden ground nearby. For a moment he took it to be some curious form of animal life peculiar to this fantastic planet—then almost immediately it dawned upon him that it was the figure of a young woman lying face downwards, most of her clothes charred and threadbare. The glow was coming from her body, so impregnated was she with radioactivity.

"Viona!" Abna's voice caught in a little gasp. Even he had never expected that prolonged absorption of radioactivity could produce such a startling 'glow-worm' effect. Then, ignoring the dangers of contamination, he hurried forward and dropped on his knees beside the sprawling figure, gathering her up in his powerful arms. In the process her face turned toward him and his horror deepened. In the normal sense there was no face left any more. It was a blurred, featureless oval, only visible at all by reason of the ghastly glow of radioactivity. Viona of the bright eyes and merry smile was nothing but a half-consumed yet still living mass of clay, as malformed by the radiations as though she were a statue which a sculptor had yet to finish.

Then Abna rose, her limp form in his arms. He could feel her pulses still faintly beating in his grasp, and the only explanation for continued life in what was nearly death was her superhuman resistance, which was fighting until the last spark was extinguished.

Abna began moving quickly, mentally battling against two enemies now—the girl's own desperate plight and his contamination from holding her. To this was added his normal, human struggle and the horror of beholding his beloved daughter reduced to a shapeless travesty of a woman.

The distance from the *Ultra* had not been great enough for him to lose touch with it, and in a short while the friendly glare of the searchlight began to appear as an aura through the mist. In the porthole the Amazon moved quickly into the pressure chamber until the airlock had been opened and closed—then she came into the control room and stared in silent horror upon Viona as she lay motionless on the wall-bunk.

"Abna, is she—"

"No, she isn't dead." Abna's handsome face was serious. "For that at least let us be thankful. She's a pretty terrifying example of the effects of uncontrolled radioactivity.... You had better keep quiet for awhile, Vi. This is going to take all the metaphysical power I possess to straighten her out, as well as restore myself. The radiation's at work on me: I can feel it."

"I'll get the *Ultra* into space," the Amazon said woodenly, and turned towards the switchboard. And thereafter, once the take-off was complete, she remained silent, watching her husband as he knelt beside the stricken girl.

An hour passed. The *Ultra* by this time had fled far from the terror world of Nur and was curving inwards in a mighty arc towards the unfathomable abode of the Mizanu. Watching that world as it came upward imperceptibly through the gulf, the Amazon set her mouth harshly. In her estimation nothing could be too diabolical as reprisal for the pitiless brain that condemned its enemies to the world of Nur.

"I believe...the struggle is over."

It was Abna's quiet voice, having within it the tautness of his mental labors. He slowly stood up, gazing upon Viona as she still lay on the bunk. The Amazon turned her attention from the porthole to look, still half expecting to see the burned, maimed wreck that Abna had brought in— But there was no such evidence. The copper-golden hair was no longer singed to the roots—it was as thick and wavy as it had always been. The blasted face was calmly reposeful, every feature perfect. The limbs of her perfect young body were resilient again, the flesh copper-tinted amidst the debris of the clothes which remained.

"Satisfied?" Abna asked, pressing finger and thumb to his eyes for a moment.

"What a prosaic question for such an achievement!" the Amazon whispered, moving forward.

Abna was silent, watching as the Amazon looked down in genuine gratitude on the restored and sleeping girl; then she glanced up sharply.

"And you? Have you put yourself right as well?"

"Yes—but it wasn't easy. The best thing now, Vi, will be first some fresh clothes in readiness for Viona when she wakes up, and after that a good meal. That much done, we'll decide on the next move."

The Amazon laughed shortly. "There's hardly any need to debate that, is there? It's perfectly obvious what our next move must be—the total destruction of that planetary brain."

"I know that, but have you yet decided how? I've been far too busy to even give it a thought. I left it to you."

"So far nothing has occurred to me—but it will."

With that she turned away and gathered together the necessary essences and concentrates for a meal. By the time she had set them out on the table, Viona was showing signs of recovery. There was an obvious dazed wonder in her sapphire blue eyes as she looked about her.

"The—the *Ultra*!" she muttered, incredulous. "How did I ever get here?"

She suddenly caught sight of her mother and father beside the table, which was enough to arouse her into a sitting position. In surprise she stared down at her rags of clothing.

"Better make yourself decent," Abna suggested, smiling—and he was met by that same incredulous stare.

"I—I can't believe that I'm really here, and safe—and well! Last thing I remember, the exhaustion of pain had overcome me. The hell world was all about me, and—"

"There is the hell world," the Amazon interrupted, and gave a brief nod towards the porthole. Through it the receding gray globe of Nur was intensely visible.

"I found you, straightened you out, and here we are," Abna said, as though his metaphysical feats were trifling. "Now get yourself properly dressed, m'dear, and then we'll have something to eat."

For answer Viona crossed to where her father was standing. She laid a gentle hand on his massive arm.

"Words aren't much use sometimes to express one's emotions, but— Well, thanks! Again and again! I've a good idea what you must have been through, and I want you to know I'm grateful."

Abna only smiled and turned away to the table.

Thereafter there was a brief interval whilst Viona hurried to her room, then in a while she was back, freshened up and attired in silk shirt and slacks.

"Makes you wonder," Abna said slowly, pondering, "what form of destruction there is that could really finish us. You know something, you two? I begin to believe that we are eternal and indestructible. The more powerful becomes one's grip on the laws of metaphysics, the greater the mastery over elemental forces. I've learned a lot on this voyage. Time and again I have had to use mental control over the physical, and it's only been that that has defeated death."

"No doubt of it," Viona agreed, taking a concentrate cube. "The drawback is that only you can do it. I tried out there on Nur, and failed utterly. And certainly mother's no good at it."

"It takes time," the Amazon said, instantly on the defensive. "Your father has been trained that way and I haven't.... In any case that is not the point at the moment. We have to work out now some kind of plan for the destruction of the Mizanu. A menace like that, and one so utterly pitiless, cannot be allowed to go on living. We, as crusaders trying to unify the Universe and form a brotherhood of interplanetary peoples, have to finish this particular mission on which we're launched. I don't doubt but what the people of Axilon will be well able to form a happy, progressive society once the Mizanu is wiped out."

"Which," Abna said, "brings us back to the original problem. How does one destroy an entire world instantly? And instantly it must be, so it does not have time to think up some form of retaliation."

CHAPTER FOURTEEN
IN MENTAL CHAINS

There a long silence; then suddenly Viona gave a little shudder. "If only there were some way to make the Mizanu feel the miseries of its victims! If it could experience the horrors of Nur, where those hapless people from Axilon died like flies on a red-hot griddle! That would be justice indeed."

"Justice indeed," the Amazon agreed, her eyes glinting. "I am glad to see, Viona, that you have the sense to nurse a spirit of revenge when a wrong has been done you. Your father probably thinks we should do nothing at all to the Mizanu...."

"I believe justice should be done, certainly," Abna replied. "But Viona's hope is a long way off the mark. To subject a whole planetary brain to the sufferings of its victims is outside the realm of practicality...." He considered for a moment; then, "That planet is about eight thousand miles in diameter, which is a pretty good mass to destroy at one blow. If we used everything we've got on the *Ultra*, we'd do no more than make a crater or two. We need an overwhelmingly powerful cosmic explosion, and even if we had the wherewithal to do that, we'd still have to consider the safety of the Axilonians. Whatever destroys the Mizanu may also reach as far as them."

"There's one thing I am wondering about," Viona said, musing. "On the journey out to Nur one of the women captives from Axilon was pretty talkative. The conversation got onto the subject of gamma rays, and to my surprise she told me that there are certain periods when the power of the Mizanu is weaker than at others. It appears that those periods coincide with an excessive outpouring of gamma rays—either from Alpha Centauri or Nur."

"Which proves what?" the Amazon questioned, frowning.

"I don't know. It just seems that the Mizanu is susceptible to gamma rays. I'd rather got the idea it might be impervious."

Abna shook his head. "No living tissue, and brain tissue least of all, can be impervious to gamma rays. There is hardly anything in the whole universe more destructive. Like your mother, though, I don't quite see the application of gamma rays to our problem—not at the moment."

"No," Viona sighed. "Neither do I. But I would like to somehow turn a defeat into a victory. I mean, I was compelled to make that journey as a prisoner, and but for it I'd never have heard of that gamma ray angle. It pointed out to me the Mizanu's 'Achilles Heel,' if only we can find a way to make use of it somehow."

"For the moment," the Amazon said, "let us consider

something practical."

She glanced through the porthole. "We have not a very great distance to go to be within range of that planetary brain. When we are, we have to act—"

"That will not be necessary. Whatever action has to be taken will be my affair, not yours."

The trio at the table started as the words reached them. They were spoken very deliberately, yet with an icy lack of feeling that made them shiver for a moment in spite of themselves.

"There!" Viona gasped, pointing. "In the corner!"

Her parents were already looking at 'it'. Not that there was anything repulsive about the presence. Indeed, it looked like a combination of man and woman, with a face that was curiously masculine and feminine combined.

"What in cosmos is it?" Abna whispered. "Some kind of hybrid combining both sexes?"

"In a way, yes." The presence came forward a little so it was plainly distinguishable in the roof lighting. It was not a ghost, either, but a perfectly solid being— and apparently of flesh and blood, too. How it had got aboard the *Ultra* in mid-space was as yet something unsolved.

"Apparently," the presence said, with dry amusement, "you do not readily recognize a composite of your three selves?"

"That's it!" Viona snapped her fingers. "It is all three of us in one, like an overlapped photograph. But—" She stopped, plumbing the depths of bewilderment.

"You must realize," the presence said, "that you three are the only example I have of your type of life. If I were to represent my own type of life, you would not comprehend it. I could, of course, present myself in the form of one of the guards, but I will not demean myself. They are of a low, primordial type, fitted only for the carrying out of orders by brute force."

Abna spoke first after a long silence. "We have been given to understand that you are an entire planetary brain—yet you appear here as a composite of us three. How are we to reconcile that?"

"That which you behold before you is nothing more than a projection, produced by the mastery of the brain's vibrations over the elements of matter. You, Abna of Jupiter, such an expert metaphysical exponent, should have grasped that."

"You mean," the Amazon questioned, "that this projection has been hurled forth by you, from your world? That in actual fact you are an entire planet?"

"I am. You have heard already the story of my evolution: how I began simply and then grew, until now I am the all-powerful Mizanu, master of Axilon and future controller of the Universe. Up to now I have taken little action against you three because I have been interested in your behavior. There will come a day when my power will reach out across the gulf to your world, so I may as well know in advance what kind of people I shall have to master. I am pleased to say I foresee no difficulty."

The presence moved slightly and then sat down on a

screwed-down chair in the corner. It was hard to realize this was only a 'manifestation', a material mouthpiece for the baleful power that still lay tens of thousands of miles distant across space.

"Yes," the presence decided, "you are amusing—but very courageous. Up to now you are quite the highest form of mentality I have encountered. You even have a fair knowledge of science."

"Of which you have had little experience as yet," the Amazon retorted venomously. "Your ruthless brutality and oppression will compel us finally to use our science to the limit, and when that happens—"

"It will not happen," the presence interrupted. "It was because I realized you were getting your mentalities to work to decide how to overcome me that I decided to act. The game of watching is over, as far as I am concerned, and I have decided that you shall be treated as the Axilonians have been—and will be again when I have readjusted myself to their rebellion...you must learn that defiance of the Mizanu is impossible."

"Is it?" Suddenly the Amazon whipped a gun from the rack close beside her and fired it. But to her amazement, the jet of destructive flame changed to a rod of ice even as she pressed the button. The point of the ice rod struck the presence in the chest, broke, and fell in javelins to the floor.

"Do I make myself clear?" the presence inquired. "You, Abna of Jupiter, have quite a good control of material things, but I am far more advanced than you. I did not turn your fire to ice, Amazon of Earth, to save the projected image: you cannot in any case harm that. I did it merely to show my control—the control that will break you. Or, better still, which will make you my servants until I grow tired of discovering how you of a far-distant world react."

The gun dropped from the Amazon's rigid fingers and she sat motionless, her eyes fixed on the 'manifestation'. In turn its eyes fixed upon her and it seemed to be through this visual medium that the far-distant brain kept her under complete control.

Abna and Viona exchanged glances; then abruptly Viona got to her feet.

"I believe you caught my mother at a disadvantage!" she declared spiritedly. "She is herself an expert in hypnosis and, had she been mentally on guard, she could have...."

"Child of Earth, be silent. You are merely tiresome. Sit down and do not move."

Viona sat down, nor did she move. She was as utterly petrified as her mother. Abna looked at the pair of them, comprehending at last that here was mental power unbelievable—a vast and coldly scientific hypnosis, the like of which he had never encountered before in his cosmic wanderings.

"You," the presence said abruptly, "are a different proposition entirely. You have made a study of metaphysics where your two companions have not. Nevertheless, I remain sanguine of my ability to rule you as I have them."

For answer Abna got to his feet and stood in majestic

silence, prepared for anything that the intellectual titan chose to fling at him.

"You will continue on your journey to my planet," the presence stated, "but you will not endeavor to devise ways of destroying me. Not that you could, in any case, but I do not even propose to give you the opportunity. Let your journey continue!"

"And if I refuse?" Abna asked coldly. "I believe that if I drove this machine far enough away from your world, there would finally come a point beyond which your influence could not reach. You have the mastery now because we are so close to your planet. Were I to put a million miles between us you would have no control over us due to the distance. You are not a movable entity, being embodied in a planet, therefore you can work only from the one point in space where you are now.... Once beyond your influence we could plot your destruction at leisure."

"Man of Jupiter, you are a fool! You cannot escape from my influence—ever! Now do as I have ordered."

Abna did not budge. Instead he answered: "I move only as my own will impels me, and it will take a stronger power than yours to change that!"

The presence got to its feet—impassive, radiating the frightful power of the intellectual monstrosity back of it. Abna could feel a tautening of his nerves, then came the baleful impact of the Mizanu's thought-waves. It felt to Abna as though he were suddenly in the midst of a smothering tide. Engulfing thoughts, none of them his own, rode into his mind and took slow possession of his faculties. Yet he still held his ground, fighting back with everything he possessed.

"You will go to that switchboard and drive your machine to my world," the presence stated implacably. "And you will do it now."

"No!" Abna shook his head and perspiration trickled down from his brow.

"Now!" the presence repeated tonelessly.

"I will not! Giant though you may be, you cannot break me down! I refuse to obey...."

Silence. Like the inexorable tightening of a thumb-screw, Abna could feel wave upon wave of mental compulsion battering against him. He stumbled; he fought in anguished silence, but with relentless inevitability he took a step toward the switchboard, then another— Then another.

"Continue your journey!" the presence said at last, and with that it melted into thin air.

Abna did not see the 'manifestation' depart. His eyes were fixed dead ahead of him toward the brain world—but they were eyes that were blank and dead. Abna, the lordly metaphysical master of Jove, had met his mental superior.

CHAPTER FIFTEEN
WORLD OF THE MIZANU

The *Ultra* landed on the world of the Mizanu an hour later—and though Abna, Viona, and the Amazon all saw the landing, and experienced all the sensations compatible with it, they had the impression that it was all a dream, that they were thousands of miles from the actual happening.

Mechanically, Abna unscrewed the airlock and opened it, then he stepped outside. A subconscious nudging told him that he should first have consulted the instruments registering external conditions, but he did not do so. As it happened, the air was breathable enough, while the temperature was about the equal of that existing on Axilon.

Without looking at each other, not speaking, and entirely unarmed, the trio started a steady march. They were leaving the *Ultra* behind them.

Abna, always able to exercise more mental control than either the Amazon or Viona, was the least submerged in the intellectual tide, and for this reason—though he was not powerful enough to exert his full individual will—he was able to absorb the details around him and wonder subconsciously at the biological marvel which had turned this planet into a brain world.

The ground he and the two women were traversing at the moment was not ground in the normal sense. It had a curious sponge-rubber quality, an amazing elasticity, which seemed to infer that it was more a hard, fleshy fiber than anything else.... And it was everywhere as far as, the eye could see—a great plain of it, ridged in places and rising up here and there into huge hummocks which could be nothing more or less than hypertrophied clusters of cells.

Abna had discovered long ago—as had the Amazon—that thought properly requires no material structure by which to express itself. This fact had been learned in Viona's sojourn to the ultimate of all intelligence. Yet here was a colossus of a material brain, the only known medium for 'interpreting' thought, believing itself to be complete master of the situation.

Trees, vegetation, the products normal to a world—these had gone. There was nothing but this everlasting plain of incredible cellular substance, its heart no doubt in the ruined city. This was the Mizanu, the superpower that had foresworn to one day dominate all the Universe.

Here and there, on their way to the city, the trio caught glimpses of small huddles of buildings that had somehow survived the tentacle claws of the vast organism, unless they had been built afterwards. It was around these dwellings that they also caught sight of living beings—ugly-faced, brutal. In fact, the same race from which had sprung the guards who ruled the helpless Axilonians.

Then there were the space-grounds. Here and there amidst the general grayness of the plateau these open spaces became visible. Upon some of them space machines were assembled, doubtless ready at a moment's notice to take off for Axilon—or any other point the Brain deemed necessary.

And still the trio marched steadily, oblivious to tiredness, hunger, or any other physical reaction. The Brain was thinking and acting for them, therefore their own individualities were pushed into the background. They entered the ruined city, traversed many of its streets—all of them choked with the ubiquitous gray cellular material, and at length came to the heart of the long dead metropolis. Here, in the center of a colossal crater, lay a stupendous hemisphere, gray, featureless, yet vibrantly alive.

The trio stopped, simply because they were commanded to do so. They stared at the amazing 'thing' incredulously.

"You gaze upon the Mizanu, travelers from afar...." The thought-waves were as distinct as spoken words. "You behold before you the seat of reason, the core of the brain which covers this entire world. And you are fools enough to think you can be defiant!"

The trio made no comment because they were incapable of it.

"You know my story, my history," the thought-waves resumed. "I was a scientist, a single individual, and destroyed my race with a blast of mental power—albeit accidentally. Some of the lowlier types remained and they have since become guards. That is my brief history. The radioactive composition of this planet fed the ever-growing cells and now you see the cumulative result."

The mental control relaxed slightly and the three vaguely wondered why; then it occurred to them it was probably so that they could make response if they wished. Since they still remained silent, the thought-waves came again, and with them a return of the full control.

"As I stated earlier through the 'manifestation' I shall be interested to observe your reactions—and, further, you need to fully understand that my power is infinitely superior to yours. Or are you satisfied already on that point? Doubtless you will recall that even the insulation around your space machine did not prevent my producing a projection within your vessel. From that alone you should appreciate how utterly impossible it is to defy me."

Abruptly, Abna made a tremendous mental effort, and held it long enough to ask a question:

"If you do not fear us, if you are so absolutely sure of your own power, why do you take the trouble to keep laboring the point? Those who are assured of mastery never even consider the other side.... You betray yourself, Mizanu. You are afraid!"

The vice-hold of the hypnosis returned, crushing

out the remaining thoughts that Abna had formed.

"I merely seek to remind you to be prudent, for your own sakes—nothing more. I observe that your mentalities are different in operation from the fools who toil on Axilon, which explains why my hypnosis did not control you while you were there. That can easily be adjusted. I have decided to send you to Axilon, where you can work with those whom you imagine you have helped. I know that they have revolted and used the neutralizing machines to temporarily suspend my power—but that state of affairs cannot last. When I have tired of observing how you react, and have learned all I need to know about you—and therefore your race—for future use, I shall destroy you. Now turn—march. Back to your ship."

Strange, even conflicting notions, passed through Abna's confused mind as he tramped on, the Amazon and Viona moving like manikins to either side of him. They reached the *Ultra* eventually and entered it mechanically, closing the airlock; then Abna turned woodenly to the switchboard. With every moment he was resentfully aware of that baleful power directing his every action.

He closed the power switches—not as he would normally have done, but as the Brain directed, and because the Brain was not familiar with the terrific power of the *Ultra*, it grossly overestimated the amount of escape velocity needed. Thinking in terms of the space machines it was accustomed to directing it classed the *Ultra* with them.

Accordingly, for the first time, the *Ultra* made the take-off at maximum power under Abna's unwilling hand—and the result of this was nearly cataclysmic. The whole stupendous energy of the copper block in the plant transferred itself to the jets and the *Ultra* literally fell at maximum speed into the sky. Tough though the plates were, they creaked dangerously under the tremendous stress thrown upon them. Here and there some of the instruments cracked as their molecular set-up was wrenched asunder— And for the three themselves, it was as if the ceiling crashed down on them and flattened them upon and through the floor.

Complete blackout crashed down on their minds. They lay flat on the floor, so tightly pressed to it they looked as though they were in bas-relief. Two seconds and the *Ultra* was beyond the Brain planet's atmosphere. Four seconds and it was a million miles away, fast approaching the incredible speed of light.

Two million miles. Three. Four. Five million.... All trace of the Brain's power was gone and the *Ultra* still flashed on with inconceivable velocity, unguided, catapulted through the awful depthless reaches of infinity.

* * * * * * *

"What in creation happened?" Viona asked, rubbing her aching forehead.

"From the look of it—plenty!" Abna stared through the porthole, and then frowned. Still frowning, he moved to the power plant and inspected it, and then finally he studied the instruments. The Amazon came across to his side.

"Exhausted," she said, looking at it. "Completely. And there was enough copper in there, under full current, to take us halfway back to Earth. Where we are and how we got here I haven't the slightest idea."

"The explanation's simple," the Amazon said. "The *Ultra*'s main computer brain is still programmed with our original flight plan for the journey to Alpha. When we neared the speed of light, it automatically cut in and took over the controls. It projected us into the fourth dimension, and we achieved supra-light velocity compared to the normal universe. Then, as the copper block became exhausted, it collapsed the energy field and we dropped back into normal space...."

"Can't see it matters much any way," Viona commented, gazing on to eternal space. "We've escaped from that overgrown genius, and that's the main thing."

"So we have...." Abna gave a little start as he remembered. Then he looked at the Amazon. "That means we must have covered a tremendous distance."

CHAPTER SIXTEEN
VIONA'S PLAN

"We'll slow down to something reasonable, then decide what comes next," Abna decided, and crossed to the spare copper blocks which the Axilonian workers had—providentially—put there in case of need. To put one in the matrix was only the work of a moment, and then Abna restored the current, this time directing the recoiling energy through the forward tubes. With the passage of time this 'braking' manoeuvre, the only one possible in space, would begin to have an effect.

Turning from the power plant, he found the Amazon immersed in mathematics as she consulted the instruments and the void.

"I do believe we're lost!" she exclaimed, astounded.

Viona said: "If the Brain thinks we're lost in space, it'll be doubly unguarded!"

"Wouldn't it be better," the Amazon asked, "if we determined how to even find the Brain world again before we start congratulating ourselves on an easy victory?"

"Probably," Viona admitted. "But it's nice to indulge in wishful thinking sometimes. Personally, I don't think we'll ever find the way back, so why not let it drop? We'll crusade somewhere else now we've got this far."

The Amazon shook her head slowly. "If I spend the rest of eternity on the job, I'll find that monstrous planet again and destroy it. As yet, from the general standard, it is only in embryo, but as time goes on its power will menace every planet in the Universe. You don't suppose it will be content with just staying chained to one planet, do you?"

"Not a case of that, is it?" Viona questioned. "It has just got to stay chained to the world on which it lives."

"By no means. Cellular material can divide itself—even transmit its cells through free space without harm. Those cells can fall on other worlds and slowly mature. That Brain can spread everywhere if we don't stop it."

"Your mother is right," Abna confirmed, as the girl looked at him. "For the sake of everything decent and the cause to which we have committed ourselves, we must find the way back and free the unhappy people of Axilon—and overcome the threat which broods over the entire Universe. As to what method of destruction we can adopt without getting too near to the Brain-world and falling in its influence again...well, I'm beaten at the moment."

"I'm not," Viona said simply, and her parents looked at her in surprise.

"You have some kind of plan?" The Amazon was looking frankly doubtful.

"Why shouldn't I have?" Viona demanded, a trifle

belligerently. "Because I'm young doesn't prevent me having inspirations, does it? The thing's pretty easy. Simply wipe the Brain-world out with concentrated gamma rays."

There was silence in the control room. Viona waited earnestly, then she looked disappointed.

"I thought I'd got a good idea. Sorry."

"It's absurd," the Amazon said, irritated. "We can't just blot out a whole planet with gamma rays—just like that! We haven't the resources, for one thing, and for another we'd never get near enough to the Brain-world without falling under its influence."

"I'm talking about Nur!" Viona slapped her hand on the table. "I told you before. That worker who told me about the Brain relaxing its power when gamma ray influence is excessive. That proves the Brain cannot stand up to concentrated gamma rays. All right so far?"

"Keep going," Abna invited.

"Nur is obviously a world in a state of extreme instability, in the process of severe mutational changes. For that reason it must be positively fluid inside and one mighty wallop would probably disintegrate it completely. If that happened there would be a dissipating deluge of gamma rays, and probably other rays besides, which would sizzle the Brain-world and everything on it to a crisp!"

"The child's right!" Abna breathed.

"To get back to the Alpha system within anything like a reasonable time," Viona said, "we'll need to reverse our journey and use fourth-dimensional transit again."

Abna shrugged. "Simple enough. All the necessary co-ordinates have been recorded and are stored in the *Ultra*'s computer brain. That does not present any problem at all. So having worked out that much, hadn't we better determine how we are to warn the Axilonians when we return?"

There was a long silence as each thought the matter out carefully.

"Lead is a possible insulator against gamma rays," the Amazon said presently. "It will even block cosmic rays, which are shorter than gamma. And Axilon is well supplied with lead in its underworld."

Abna nodded slowly. "By this time let's hope most of them have taken our advice and made helmets out of the stuff. The only suggestion I can think of is to have them build vast numbers of lead shelters and stay within them at the zero hour, or at least until they get our signal that the gamma radiation has dissipated."

"And how do we do that?" Viona asked pointedly. "They don't know anything about radio, and that's our only means of keeping in touch from a distance. If we supply them with a radio set it will mean coming within range of the planetary-brain. I don't say he will be expecting us, but I doubt if we'll escape his notice."

"Definitely a problem," Abna sighed. "I was going to say we might keep in touch by mental telepathy. I could single out one trustworthy worker for the job, but even that would not work because it would mean that particular worker would have to be without a lead helmet, and the influence of the Mizanu would swamp my own mental communication...."

"Only one way," the Amazon said at last. "One of us must descend on Axilon and hope that the Mizanu does not witness the occurrence. The remaining two will deal with the destruction of Nur and the consequent destruction of the planet-brain."

"I'll go to Axilon," Viona volunteered promptly. "Be more fun to me than watching you old-stagers destroying a planet. I'll get some exercise, too. I feel too cooped-up in the *Ultra* all the time."

The Amazon shrugged. "Immaterial which of us goes, but I should dissuade myself from the idea that you are going to have a happy holiday. There'll be grim danger every moment—the danger that the Mizanu will detect you."

"Even if he does, he can only put me to work, as he intended doing with all of us. Anyhow, I'm not scared." Viona's blue eyes were bright with excitement again. "When I get to Axilon, what do I do?"

"Keep yourself alert for my mental communications," Abna answered. 'You'll be without a lead helmet and will stay without one since—unless you're detected—the Mizanu's mental wavelength will not affect you. I'll mentally advise you of everything your mother and I are doing, and you in turn can direct the Axilonians to safety. It's a big assignment, m'dear. Think you can handle it?"

Viona laughed. "Nothing easier—providing that the Mizanu has not succeeded overcoming the rebellion in the meantime. He did say something about getting it under control."

"No plan is perfect," Abna said philosophically. "We'll have to take a chance on that.... Right, then, we'll drop you on Axilon as unobtrusively as possible, and after that you'll be on your own until we can pick you up again. The telepathy will not be one-sided either. You must advise me when the lead shelters are ready, since nothing can be done with Nur until they are."

"Everything will be all right; rely on me."

"Which leaves us with the final point," the Amazon commented. "How to destroy Nur, eight thousand miles in diameter."

Again the spell of thought, then Abna turned and studied the *Ultra*'s weapons. Finally he shook his head.

"We've nothing powerful enough there to create an instantaneous explosion sufficient to blow Nur to pieces. Even if we dumped every explosive we've got on Nur and then supplied them with delayed-action fuses so they'd all explode simultaneously, I don't think we'd produce anything more than a dent."

Again the silence, but no conclusion seemed to be reached. Finally Abna got up from the table and looked down on the two women seriously.

"Something will probably occur to us by the time it's needed. It's very rare for us to find a barrier we can't hurdle."

With that he turned again to the switchboard and took a reading. Their speed had dropped amazingly and was now well below that of light-velocity.

"You two had better get some rest," Abna said, glancing across. "We'll be a while yet before we can turn the *Ultra* around and commence the return journey, so get some sleep while you can. I'll wake you fast enough if anything unusual happens."

CHAPTER SEVENTEEN
THE ASTEROID

It was three hours later when the Amazon suddenly found herself aroused from slumber by the harsh stridence of the alarm system.

Since this was self-operated and controlled by radar, the radar-echo setting off the alarm the moment it struck anything well in advance of the *Ultra*, it meant that Abna himself was not responsible.

In a matter of seconds the Amazon was fully awake and prepared for any emergency. She hurried quickly into her black space kit, glanced outside on the eternal stars and beheld nothing unusual, and then she whipped open the door of the bedchamber. Viona was speeding down the corridor and she slithered to a standstill as she beheld her mother.

"Father playing games, do you suppose?" she asked quickly. "I wouldn't put it past him."

"Not on this occasion, Viona. It's the advance alarm system in action. Something must be ahead of us."

They hurried on quickly into the control room to find Abna at the telescopic equipment, intently studying the reflector plate. At the sound of the two women's footfalls he turned quickly.

"Something about a million miles in front of us," he announced, "and at the speed we're going at we'll reach it very quickly. I'm trying to discover what it is, but there's no sign of anything. I don't see that it can be a black hole, otherwise we'd feel the gravity-pull, and the instruments don't register anything at all. It's not excessively large, whatever it is...." He broke off and gave an exclamation. "I see it! Look!"

He indicated the reflector-plate quickly. The two women looked intently on a rugged, uneven mass blotting out the stars ahead. Since there were no near stars at this point in space, the dark object was not even faintly illuminated. The only sign of its presence at all was revealed by the starry area that it was engulfing.

"It's a meteoroid," the Amazon said. "That's the only explanation. One of the interstellar variety, which has drifted across our course."

"Far more than a meteoroid," Viona corrected, looking at the computing instruments. "Look at the size of it! Close on 3,000 miles across! It's a large asteroid—"

"And coming close mighty fast!" Abna darted across to the control board and set to work to swerve the *Ultra*'s headlong flight clear of the ponderously moving hulk. If a collision occurred with it, the impact would probably smash the *Ultra*'s armor-plating, densely thick though it was.

By this time, thanks to the space machine's velocity, the wandering asteroid was visible to the naked eye through the portholes—or rather its presence was noticeable by the black irregular lake swallowing up the stars. With the seconds it became larger, but swinging away to the right now as Abna carefully changed course to avoid collision and match velocity with it.

"I've got an idea!" Viona gasped suddenly, twirling on her heel. "If only it will work—"

"Keep it 'til later," Abna said tensely. "I've no time to listen with this asteroid nearly on top of us—"

"But that's just it!" Viona was nearly dancing with excitement. "Can you anchor it somehow? Tow it along with us?"

"What in cosmos for?"

"For use later as a sort of battering ram to hurl at Nur! If we could get enough velocity behind the asteroid, we could make good use of it!"

"It's a stroke of genius!" the Amazon exclaimed. "No reason why we can't do it, Abna. The asteroid's wandering free and is quite unchained. We'll get a pull back as we throw the power into the attractors but once we've got the hulk in our grip, it will follow us without resistance with no major gravity to impede it. And it can easily be encompassed within our four-dimensional field when we commence the return journey to the Alphan system."

Abna only nodded; he had too much on his mind to indulge in actual words. Carefully he watched his chance, then as at last the huge bulk fled past at a safe distance he threw in the power of the *Ultra*'s rear attractors. From them there immediately radiated that magnetism, which was capable of chaining anything with a metallic content. Evidently the asteroid had such a content, for the *Ultra* immediately jerked violently like a fast-moving vehicle suddenly held by an unbreakable chain.

The power plant hummed and whined, dangerously close to breakdown as it struggled to accustom itself to the sudden and unexpected extra load.

"It'll make it," the Amazon whispered, her eyes fixed on the instruments. "I know the strength of that plant."

So did Abna, but even so both of them wondered for a moment or two if they had attempted too much. The *Ultra* had not stopped its advance at high speed; it had merely been slowed down. It was now a toss-up whether it would slowly regain its original velocity and drag the hulk along with it, or whether the mass gravity of the hulk would prove too much and cause the power plant to race itself to pieces. If that happened—

"We're doing it!" It was Viona's bated voice as she beat her fists excitedly on the porthole rim. "The hulk's trailing along to rearward, keeping its distance, and our speed is slowly increasing again."

This was a fact and in a few more minutes the battle was over. The overstrained humming of the power plant subsided to the normal buzzing and the *Ultra*'s velocity returned to what it had been before the check. A mile to rearward hung the great mass of abandoned rock, all 3,000 miles of it, held immovably by the attractors.

Once he was back on the original course, however, Abna cut out the attractors as superfluous—and the great asteroid still kept pace with them at the same distance, having now fallen into an organized gravity field. It was a case of the midget pulling the giant, and the chain between them was the invisible one of gravity.

* * * * * * *

Hours passed and, as before, the *Ultra* built up velocity to just under that of light, and then the vessel and its companion body was enveloped in the four-dimensional field generated automatically by the computer brain and power plant. This meant that both the *Ultra* and the asteroid were traveling at supra-light velocity compared to the normal universe outside the warp field. And this hour upon hour and hour upon hour, meant that the enormous distance to the region of Alpha Centauri at last began to lessen appreciably—and even as Abna had said, the course was exactly a straight line as before, so they were compelled to return to the point from which they had started, but with the difference that in the meantime the entire mass of the Universe had turned slowly on its great, imponderable axis, thereby creating a different angle of approach to the Alpha Centauri system. Not that this signified. Just as long as Alpha himself was visible, the rest was simple.

And indeed Alpha was at last visible, though the three inside the space machine were still lost in the depths of unconsciousness. Alpha first appeared as a pinpoint in the abysmal deeps, and thereafter grew with awesome, frightening speed—gradually becoming obvious as a binary when Proxima, the eternal companion of the starry giant, also assumed visible proportions.

Since everything was perfectly calculated, the copper block in the power plant expended itself in almost the same time as its predecessor on the outward journey, the fractional discrepancy in time being accounted for by the time lag in anchoring the hulk. This meant that the *Ultra* dropped into normal space sooner than Abna had calculated, which was all to the good, for he awoke to weightless conditions to find Alpha Centauri and the attendant worlds perilously close.

Immediately he propelled himself to the switchboard and cut in the artificial gravity. Then he hurriedly replenished the power plant with more copper and switched on the forward tubes to maximum. Even so, it was plain it would be touch and go whether the vast speed could be mastered quickly enough to prevent the vessel sailing far beyond the Alpha system—or worse still, being unable to turn aside in time and instead be caught by huge Alpha's gravity and be dragged into him.

Silent, his handsome face shadowed with doubts, Abna watched the fast-approaching system; then he became aware that the awakened Amazon and Viona were at his side.

"We made it, then?" Viona asked brightly.

"Yes—and rather too successfully, I'm afraid. I only

hope we can turn aside in time. At the moment I can't move the ship's nose away from the course because our velocity is too high."

With that he returned to the switches and watched the red guider needle intently. It was still exactly at the vertical, overlaying the course indicator needle, which meant that as yet no divergence to one side had been made. And the tens of thousands of miles were flashing by in the split seconds.

Thousands of miles vanished and the needle flickered again, this time showing a much more noticeable divergence from the vertical—and what was more significant, it held the position. Through the portholes the Alpha system was only a matter of 6,000,000 miles distant. Soon the three planets themselves would be visible.

The guider needle struggled further over to the left, leaving a V-shaped segment between itself and the course indicator line.

"We're doing it," Abna whispered, his face drawn with strain. "And not a second too soon either. Yes, I can move her now. She's manoeuvrable again, and we're well below the velocity of light now. Yes, we'll be okay. Viona, how's the hulk getting on?"

"Still in step." Viona looked through the rearward prism. "Since it's now anchored to use by rods of force, it's also affected by our own deceleration. Keep on like that as long as we wish it to."

The vessel under complete control at last, Abna relaxed a trifle and surveyed the distant Alpha system pensively. Then finally he looked at Viona.

"Viona, we now face the problem of getting you to Axilon without making ourselves conspicuous—and we'll be more conspicuous than ever with this hulk chained to us. In fact, it is perfectly obvious that as far as the *Ultra* is concerned, no landing can he attempted anywhere while this hulk is near us. It would crush us completely due to the gravity pull."

"All of which your bright little daughter has already thought out!" Viona spread her hands. "What I am going to do is use the small emergency escape ship, by which I ought to avoid all observation."

"Yes, it's about the best way," the Amazon admitted.

CHAPTER EIGHTEEN
VIONA IN THRALL

It was an hour later when at length the correct position in space had been attained, and without any interruption from the Brain-planet, either. And here, with the speed slowed almost to zero, the task of remaining 'stationary' in space, and also keeping the hulk at a respectable distance, became a matter of celestial mathematics. It meant jockeying into position, even receding from Nur itself, until that planet's gravitational field no longer set up an appreciable disturbing influence. As a final result, the *Ultra* came to a 'standstill' at approximately a million miles from Nur, there to remain until the circumstances warranted the dispatch of the hulk to destroy the radioactive planet.

The Amazon created a 'cloaking' field of energy around the *Ultra* and the asteroid, by which light and radar waves were diverted around it—except for a narrow channel through which those in the *Ultra* could see out—rendering it almost invisible. They were still detectable because of the asteroid's gravitational mass, but it was unlikely that any of the Mizanu's minions would be operating the necessary instruments to detect the change in the gravitational equilibrium of the Alphan system. They had no reason to suspect anything.

"Which means there's nothing for it now but waiting and watching," Abna sighed, gazing through the port once more. "And that is always the hardest thing to do.... Maybe I should spend most of my time relaxed. I'll be better able that way to sense Viona's concentration when she communicates."

"No sign of anything so far, I suppose?" the Amazon asked.

"Not yet. I hardly expect it. She'll have to orientate herself even when she has landed—granting the Brain does not grab her."

The Amazon frowned with momentary anxiety, then with a shrug she turned to the instruments and began to busy herself with a maze of equations. Abna frowned as he watched her.

"Why all that? We're perched safely enough here with gravities counterpoised, aren't we?"

"That isn't the problem now." The Amazon glanced up briefly. "I'm working out how we can hurl this hulk at Nur and yet pull free ourselves. We've got to know exactly what we're doing when we do start, otherwise we'll be in monumental danger of crashing.... That doesn't mean that you need to lend a hand, though. I'm perfectly capable of working this out by myself. You keep your mind clear in readiness for Viona."

Viona, in the meantime, had, to her considerable surprise and relief, made the landing on Axilon without mishap. She put down her escape from the planet-brain's attentions to the fact that the emergency projectile was so small it could hardly have been seen telescopically from the brain-world. She had approached the planet at such an angle and speed that the planet's atmosphere had slowed her descent with minimal use of breaking rocket-bursts. On the other hand, since it was physically impossible for the Brain itself to use telescopic equipment, the immunity from interference might lie in the fact that it was not expecting to ever see the three from far-off Earth again, and therefore the solitary mind of Viona had not made as much as a ripple in the vast pitiless intellect which ruled the Alpha system.

Whatever the answer, Viona was as yet unharmed, and brought her machine down on the outskirts of the slave city where she and her parents had begun their Axilonian adventure. Just as she had expected, she had only covered a dozen yards from her vessel, her gun ready in her hand, when she beheld a party of workmen coming toward her, themselves carrying weapons. For a moment she could not decide why they looked so odd—just like old photographs she had once seen of Germans in a far-gone World War II; then it occurred to her it was the lead helmets that conveyed this impression.

Approaching more closely, the leader of the workers gave the signal to his colleagues to lower their guns, then he came forward with hand extended in greeting.

"Welcome back, comrade, from a far world. We had been wondering what had happened to you since your parents departed to find you on Nur—" The worker glanced about him. "But where are they? Why is your space machine so small?"

"They are somewhere near Nur," Viona answered. "That space machine is only an emergency one. I had to come here as secretly as possible in case the Mizanu detected me. I have much to arrange with you, so please listen carefully."

"Willingly. It will be more comfortable at our head-quarters, though. Come along with us."

Viona nodded and fell into step with the guards. Those who had never seen her before gave her covert glances, but apparently their leader was already acquainted with the three from Earth, even though Viona herself could not recall having seen him before.

"How does the rebellion progress?" she inquired, as they made good speed toward the slave city.

"Excellently, thanks to the advice given us by your mother and father. We lost no time in securing lead and fashioning rough helmets, which you see us now wearing. If the hypnosis neutralizers should be put out of action—which so far they have not been—we shall remain uncontrolled by the Mizanu. As for the rebellion itself, it has now spread through three-quarters of our world. There being a considerable supply of lead throughout the planet, helmets are being made in the tens of thousands. But though they give us immunity from the Mizanu, they do not unfortunately contribute anything to his overthrow."

"That is our task," Viona replied. "And that is why

I am here. By 'our' task, I mean that of my father, mother, and myself."

And, once the headquarters in the city were reached, she wasted no time in explaining what was intended. She did not give the details only to the few guards who had met her spaceship, but to the great crowd of helmeted men and women who had been gathered together specially to hear her.

Surveying the interested but uncomprehending workers as she talked, Viona could not help but realize how little they understood the scientific implications. Her explanation of how it was intended to smash Nur to pieces with a small asteroid was clearly quite beyond comprehension. The unscientific Axilonians simply gazed like children watching a conjuring trick.

"I do not ask any of you to join in the scientific activity concerned with the Mizanu's destruction," Viona concluded. "That is left to us of the distant Earth. We said a long time ago that the Mizanu would find our science a power to reckon with, and the critical moment is not far away. What you have to do is protect yourselves against the onslaught when it comes, and the only way to do that is to build yourselves lead shelters as quickly as possible."

"That," said the leader of the workers, "should not be too difficult. We have all the labor we need, and we know that we can trust you of Earth,"

"The alternative to building shelters—and by far the quicker way if it can be done—is to go underground to regions which you know are heavily surrounded with lead, and there to stop until I give you the word that all is well for you to emerge to the surface again. If, though, the lead underground is close beside an area of radioactivity, it must not be used. The danger would be worse than ever. You understand your planet's internal formation better than I do, so what is your suggestion?"

"We can use certain areas," the leader said, after thinking for a while. "In fact, many thousands can be accommodated below, but we shall also need shelters.... You are prepared to leave it to me to make the necessary arrangements and contacts so our people can be safeguarded?"

"That is exactly what I want you to do, and your entire planet must be included. Not a single part of it is likely to escape the overflowing radiations of gamma rays when Nur is destroyed. The one-quarter of this world which is still under the Mizanus domination must be quickly brought under your own control and neutralized against the hypnosis."

"That will be done, and—"

The guard paused and stared at Viona in surprise. The vital animation of her personality had mysteriously evaporated, as had her intense concentration upon her subject. Instead she was gazing straight out before her, suddenly finding herself battling against overwhelming waves of compulsion. Even as she did so, fighting with everything she had in her, there merged into view an exact duplicate of herself, attired identically, standing not half a dozen yards away. Immediately the workers moved back hurriedly, staring in fascination at what they at first believed was a scientific dimensional miracle produced by the Earth-girl herself. It was only as the apparition spoke in a hard, mechanical voice that they realized the facts.

"Woman of Earth, your mental vibrations have just reached me—the Mizanu—and I speak to you through a projection of yourself. I was unfortunate in not detecting you quickly enough to hear your speech to these fools of workers, but I am quite convinced that you are on Axilon for no good purpose—as far as my control is concerned. Thanks to you and your two colleagues I have not yet succeeded in mastering the revolutionaries—but I shall. That can wait for the moment; my demand is to know why you are on Axilon again, when you returned from outer space, and particularly where your colleagues are. Now answer me!"

Viona remained silent. In awe the workers stared at her, then at the apparition. It was a few moments before it dawned on them that the dreaded Mizanu was back of the manifestation, but once this fact penetrated there was a growing murmur of anger.

"It is the Mizanu!" one of the workers shouted. "It has overpowered the Earth woman with hypnosis, operating through that projected image! Destroy it!"

"Kill it!"

"Break the Mizanu's power!"

Instantly the workers surged forward and, though their weapons were of the most ordinary kind—for they had not the least idea how to operate the ray-guns which had been taken from various captor-guards—

they did their best to destroy the image of Viona as she stood coldly impassive a few yards away. They threw her to the ground, battered at her with their weapons, fired very primitive bullets into her...but when at length they withdrew they discovered that, though the image's clothes were torn, the image itself was unharmed. Not a mark; not a scratch, and as though jerked by strings Viona II stood on her feet again.

Viona herself watched all this and, though deeply in the grip of hypnosis, had enough individual will left to know what would really give her the protection she needed. A lead helmet! But when she tried to put the request into words she found her tongue incapable of speaking. She could still do nothing but gaze fixedly in front of her.

"Since it will evidently be difficult for me to obtain from you what I desire, with so many revolutionaries around you," her image resumed, "I shall deal with you on my own world. Go to your space machine immediately and make the journey!"

Viona hesitated, struggling with mental helplessness against the power embracing her. She knew even as she battled that she could not win. Even her father, master of metaphysics, had failed, so what chance did she stand?

"Do—as—you—are told!"

Viona began moving slowly, placing one foot before the other with ponderous deliberation, her hands at her sides and her eyes fixed dead ahead. Some of the workers hesitated as though wondering whether or not to restrain her. But their fear of the Mizanu was too great to allow them to put their promptings into action—so they just watched fixedly as Viona walked deliberately from their midst. And hardly had she gone from amongst them before the image that had given the directions snapped into extinction.

CHAPTER NINETEEN
VIONA FIGHTS BACK

Still moving at the same robot-like pace, Viona grad-ually left the city behind and returned with mechan-ical steps to the emergency machine. She had by now ceased to exercise any effort to master the hypnosis gripping her, but that did not prevent her subconscious realization of the fact that she was now powerless to send any telepathic communication to her father, and without it he would be in a considerable dilemma.

All definitely useless speculation as far as Viona was concerned. She entered the emergency machine, closed the airlock, and then lay flat on her face on the floor, the only way in which she could travel in such narrow limits. Gazing blindly through the forward port she closed the main switches and the vessel immediately lifted, streaking out towards the looming gray mass of the planet-brain world.

How long the journey took she did not know, for her conception of time was completely dulled. She only knew that the brain-world gradually grew larger in the gulf, and that she moved the switches that gave her a safe landing on the peculiarly spongy surface of the planet.

This done, she opened the airlock and stepped outside. Immediately the force that had been ruling her seemed to increase its power and, as though seized with actual hands, she found herself turned about and impelled forward. She marched steadily until finally she reached that great crater where lay the pulsing hemisphere which was the core of the brain world. And as on that earlier occasion she could sense the battering of mental waves against her.

"I have been endeavoring, woman of Earth, to mentally locate where your two colleagues—or rather your parents—are. Since you were flung with them into outer space when I lost control of you, it is logical to assume that they returned when you did.... Why did they not go to Axilon with you? Are they alive or not?"

Viona was silent.

"I do not propose to be balked, Earth woman! Where are your parents?"

"In—in space," Viona gasped.

"That does not answer the question!"

Viona shook her head dumbly. Then she gave a little cry, again clapped her hands to her outraged head, and then collapsed on the crater's edge....

* * * * * * *

"It is strange," Abna said, frowning, "that Viona does not send any communication. It's forty-eight hours since she must have landed on Axilon."

The Amazon said: "There may be a dozen and one

reasons why Viona can't communicate. The other alternative is to try to mentally locate her—as you did when she was stranded on Nur. Can that be done?"

"I'll try."

And Abna did. Closing his eyes he remained motionless before the huge window and, in that singular way he had, gradually lost himself in concentration. The Amazon waited, completely quiet, doing nothing to disturb him.

"She's alive," he said presently. "I can sense that much—but judging from the strength of the mental radiation, she is somewhere much nearer than Axilon...."

"The only place nearest is the brain-planet itself!" the Amazon said.

She turned to the telescopic equipment and focused it upon distant Axilon. Using the ultimate in magnification, she studied the slave-planet's surface carefully and then gave a sigh.

"No sign of anything happening there. For that matter, we don't know if Viona had time to tell them to build lead shelters. We'll only know about that when sufficient time has elapsed for them to have done something we can see. Until then...." The Amazon stopped indecisively, biting her lip.

"We haven't even an emergency vessel with which to nip down to Axilon and see if the people know what's coming," Abna said. "We're just stuck in one very uncomfortable corner.... There is a solution somewhere, because there always is. The only one I can think of at the moment is to try and pinpoint exactly where Viona is and then transfer myself by mental projection to her side. The risk will be considerable and I might get myself destroyed doing it—"

"There's no 'might' about it," the Amazon interrupted. "Wherever you project yourself to on the brain-world, it will instantly seize upon you—destroy you if at all possible. We're not taking that risk. Weighed in the balances, you are far more important than Viona."

"In accomplishments, yes, but Great Heavens, Vi, you're not suggesting we make no attempt to save Viona, are you?"

The Amazon hesitated, her beautiful face clearly expressing her immense indecision. Then gradually her mouth tightened.

"If somebody has to be sacrificed, it must be Viona, the least important of our little band of three."

"But, Vi, she's our daughter and—"

"Do you think I don't realize that?" The Amazon's voice was harsh with emotional strain. "Whatever personal sentiments we have in this business have got to be eclipsed by one fact—namely, that it is more important for this brain-monstrosity to be destroyed than it is for Viona to be rescued. We have our mission to carry out, no matter what."

Abna was forced at last to a reluctant acquiescence. "Not often I agree with you, Vi, as far as Viona is concerned—but this time I've got to. Perhaps something will turn up before we need to go into action. We'll keep a constant watch on both Axilon and the brain-planet."

"And keep Viona mentally 'tuned in' as well. At least we'll have some idea from that if she's still alive."

So it was decided and thereafter the "waiting and watching" game was intensified in its strain because of the plight of Viona. But at least she was alive. The passing hours revealed that quite clearly to Abna. And, whilst she was alive, something ought surely to be possible to save her? To this end he devoted every scrap of high-level intellect, turning over idea after idea in his mind.

* * * * * * *

Four days later, by Earth-time, there came a change in the monotony. The face of Axilon was becoming marked out in a curious patchwork of gray squares. Under the fine focus of the telescope they revealed themselves clearly as squat cubes with one small opening each, presumably a door. Around them, visible as energetically moving specks, were the busy forms of the Axilonians themselves.

"That's one relief anyway," the Amazon said, when Abna had also studied the scene carefully. "They're quickly erecting tens of thousands of lead shelters. That means that Viona must have had the opportunity to tell them what to do before she was presumably snatched away to the brain-world—"

"And it also looks as though the Mizanu is not aware of the purpose of those shelters, otherwise he would have made a move by now to destroy them. Possibly even," Abna continued slowly, "the Mizanu is trying to learn from Viona why she returned from Axilon."

The Amazon nodded, her face grim. "Which will mean a good deal of mental torture for Viona. It's even doubtful if she'll be able to withstand the brain's demands.... What is your latest mental reaction concerning her?"

"Very confused. There's no doubt that she has recovered consciousness, but with the Mizanit dominating her mind it's difficult to judge her own reactions. I get glimpses of frustration, obstinacy, immense exhaustion, and hunger, but never once of fear. Even now, evidently fighting the brain-world all by herself, Viona is not afraid."

No; Viona was not afraid, but she was perilously close to extreme exhaustion. So far, following her initial breakdown before the onslaught of the Brain's probing efforts, she had succeeded in withstanding the demands hurled at her. But for four Earth-days and nights she had been without food or drink, and with only the rest that unconsciousness had given. Sleep had been and still was impossible. She lay on the edge of the crater, which contained the core of the Brain, stirring only when the angry mental lashings of the frustrated monster barbed deep within her.

"At least, woman of Earth, I compliment you on your courage," the Brain communicated, on the fourth night, as Viona lay nearly prostrate with weariness under the impersonal stars. "I have tried by the limit of mental compulsion to make you tell me where your parents are and the reason for your visit to Axilon. Since I have failed by mental means, I shall use physical force."

"That is impossible," Viona whispered indistinctly, her eyes half closed. "Such as you cannot resort to physical force."

"Those whom I rule can. You shall see."

Viona relaxed, not caring, her mind utterly numbed— but she stirred presently and looked up as the sound of footfalls reached her.

She beheld four of the brute-men who acted as guards on Axilon advancing towards her. So much she had just grasped when they reached her and dragged her to her feet. She hung heavily in their grasp, too mentally drugged to make any effort to save herself.

"There are two questions this Earth-woman must answer...." Viona could feel the mental orders being radiated to the guards. "She must say where her parents are, and she must also explain the reason for her visit to Axilon. I cannot get any information from that planet to explain the reason for the grayish squares which have recently come into being. Make her speak!"

The order was entirely to the taste of the guards' sadistic natures. At the end of ten minutes Viona was limp in their grasp, her face and body numbed and cut from a dozen merciless blows. But she still had not uttered a word.

"Possibly the woman cannot speak because of my domination over her mind...." The Brain seemed to be considering this. Then, "Whilst you have her in your grasp she cannot escape, so I can temporarily with-draw my hold over her so she can answer. Try again!"

The sudden lifting of that dreadful, deadening power which had been clamping her down for nearly five days and nights was to Viona an amazing thing. Her own individuality and control of herself abruptly returned. With it her crushing lassitude faded and, though she was ravenously hungry and parched from thirst, she was no longer on the verge of near collapse. She was her own mistress again, and that was the vital point.

For all that, she remained silent as the guards again began to go to work on her. A savage blow struck across her bruised face; a heavy boot lashed brutally at her ankle; a hand seized her left wrist and twisted her arm inexorably up her back—then with devastating speed Viona hit back.

She spun around on the man twisting her wrist and smashed up her left fist with all her strength. He yelled at the pain of his broken jaw, staggered backwards, then fell heavily into the crater containing the hemisphere of Brain. This very fact was sufficient to disturb the Brain into a violent fear for its own safety. A severe blow on any part of that essentially neuronic structure could produce devastating effects.

Not that this concerned Viona. She realized that the Brain was more concerned for its own safety than anything else at the moment so, with what strength remained to her—and that, even in her exhausted condition, was far beyond anything possessed by any normal woman in the prime of health—she lashed out left and right at her tormentors.

CHAPTER TWENTY
COSMIC COLLISION

Strong men though they were, they could not match her agility or hitting power. The second man went down with a streaming nose and a broken arm. The third and fourth leaped, and found the girl was not there. Instead, she was behind them. In one jump she was between them, locking her arms round the backs of the men's necks and then dragging inwards with all the muscular power she possessed. Here indeed she emulated exactly, without realizing it, the fatal hold so often used by her fantastic mother. Her arms drew tighter and tighter even though the struggles of the men lifted her from her feet. At last she had her fingers interlocked across her chest...and this for the men was the finish. She tightened the grip and held it, held it until no more breath could be sucked into the men's throats, until the blood circulation to their brains was completely strangled.

One dropped; then the other. Viona relaxed, drawing a forearm over the perspiration streaming down her face. She could feel the mental turmoil of the Brain as it endeavored by mental compulsion to force the fallen guard from the crater into which he had dropped. The broken jaw had blacked him out for the time being, so he just lay, his feet thrust into the delicate tissue substance, which doubtless caused the Brain not a little anguish.

Viona did not wait for any more. Finding no compulsion was being used directly upon her, she ran as fast as she could go in the direction of the emergency vessel. As far as her cloudy remembrance could help her, it lay perhaps a mile and a half away. She had to find it—and before the Brain nailed her down.

The machine loomed up dimly at last under the stars, just as she had left it. Frantically she hurried for the open airlock—just as iron mental commands voiced down upon her. She halted in her tracks, stunned by the intensity of resumed hypnosis.

"Return to me, woman of Earth! Return! Return!"

Viona remained motionless, breathing hard. Evidently the Brain had discovered her departure and, its own worries notwithstanding, had reached out to stop her. If she gave way now, it was the finish. She would never recover the initiative.

The airlock was no more than six feet away. She stared at it dazedly in the starlight.

"Return!" The command roared and battered down the corridors of her aching mind. But, deep down within her, was the age-old law of self-preservation, stronger than any command the Brain could utter. She did not meekly turn around and walk back to certain death: instead she threw the last shreds of her physical and mental power into a forward effort. She advanced, step by step. She touched the cold edges of the airlock and battled with frantic anguish against the clawing mental fingers striving to pull her back.

She dragged herself through the airlock as though weighed down by countless tons. Stupidly she slammed the airlock shut behind her and collapsed on the floor. In here, thanks to the insulation, the mental compulsion was slightly lessened.

Her quivering hand reached out and closed the main power switch. The small power plant hummed and in a sudden burst of exhaust the vessel took off toward the stars. Viona watched them through dimming eyes, her brain reeling now under the awful fury of the planet Brain's hatred. It had detected the machine's departure and its malice knew no frontiers. Lashed, scourged, battered mentally and physically, Viona could take no more.

With a low moan she collapsed into darkness and peace—and the emergency machine, uncontrolled and its power plant operating at maximum, flashed out into the deeps of space—

But not unobserved. Both Abna and the Amazon saw the tiny pinprick of light hurtling outwards from the limb of the brain-planet. In turns they watched it intently through the telescope until there was no longer any doubt.

"It's the emergency machine!" the Amazon exclaimed, startled. "Since the plant is operating, Viona must be inside. Can't be anybody else because she's the only one who understands it! Why doesn't she communicate, I wonder?"

"Probably blacked out at the rate she's going, and her speed is evidently so she can escape the compulsion of the brain-world." Abna surveyed the hurtling emergency machine through the window and then turned back to the Amazon. "She won't hit anything in the direction she's taking and we'll catch up with her later.... Which means we're not waiting any longer, Vi. Judging from the look of Axilon, most of the planet has its crude lead shelters ready. Those who can survive, will. We've got to act."

The Amazon nodded quickly. "I'm ready when you are."

She turned to the control board while Abna took charge of the magnetic attractor equipment. Both of them knew from previous rehearsal exactly what they were going to do, and mathematics had shown they could get away with it.... So the *Ultra* began to move, building up speed as quickly as possible as it hurtled in the direction of radioactive Nur. Inevitably the hulk followed in the rear, keeping exact pace.

Her every nerve geared to the task, the Amazon increased the velocity until they were within 5,000 miles of the radioactive world's surface and well inside his gravitational field. Then she abruptly cut off the attractor-beams trained on the asteroid, and used the retarder rockets and side jets. Instantly, the *Ultra* changed direction and shot off diagonally.... But mathematics had not been wrong. Chained by Nur's gravity, the stronger power, the hulk went on in a straight line, down toward that gray, inscrutable world.

The *Ultra* strained and shivered under the combined pull of both Nur and the hulk, but by using the power-plant to maximum and trusting to the mathematics which had shown the strain could be overcome, the Amazon gradually forced the vessel round in a mighty arc until it was facing the way it had come. Then, regardless of the pressures produced by extreme velocity, she hurtled the vessel out into the deeps as fast as it could possibly go—until the explosion of Nur momentarily arrested her efforts.

Abna pressed a switch and radiation-proof shields—transparent nonetheless—shot across the portholes. Through them he and the Amazon stared upon a disintegrating world and, for all their scientific imagination, they had never anticipated it could look like this.

The instant the hulk struck Nur, traveling at thousands of miles an hour, the unstable, rotten planet smashed like an eggshell. Light of blinding intensity flared into the void, the core of which contained fast dissipating waves of deadly energy. They were moving outward at the speed of light and must have engulfed the planet-brain in a matter of seconds. They overtook the *Ultra* and set the instrument's needles dancing, but they did not penetrate the proofed walls since their power was already weakening.... Viona's machine they would never reach in strength, for she was a million miles and more away by now.

"Let us see what happened," Abna said at last, when

the cataclysmic disturbance had quieted into a mighty sea of cosmic debris.

He turned to the telescope and looked long and earnestly on the Alpha system as it slowly sped away from them. Then the Amazon took his place and intently studied a brown, blistered planet that had been a brain. Nowhere was there a living cell left. The gamma rays had reduced that stupendous neuronic tissue to charred, flaky dust, and even revealed glimpses of barren but normal planet beneath. Intensely radioactive as yet, but in time....

"Well, the job's done," Abna said at last. "Axilon seems in reasonable shape, so it's a safe bet that the majority of the folks survived under their lead shelters. Enough of them anyway to build up an ordered society freed from that monstrous oppressor."

"We could go back and see," the Amazon said, turning to the switchboard.

"We could—but why? We've done our job and we have no part in their society. Besides, there must be other tasks awaiting us as Crusaders—way out there."

He nodded to the vast deeps beyond Alpha; then abruptly he swung his attention back to the telescope. For a long time he peered through it, circling it around the great dome which gave an uninterrupted view of all sides.

"There she is!" he cried at length. "Viona's still going. Keep up this pace and we'll catch her in thirty minutes."

"And if she's dead?" the Amazon asked grimly.

"She isn't. I can sense her mind is still alive, which means she is. She's done a great job, and suffered plenty. But no matter, it will make her a seasoned pioneer...." Abna broke off and grinned. "Once she's back with us we'll celebrate, and then back to business. We've started a good cause by freeing the Axilonians. There must be other problems in the eternal depths of space. Perhaps even out there in the great Milky Way Galaxy. I've often wondered what kind of people spawn in those starry oceans. Have they dreams, hopes, and ambitions, like us?"

"If they're alive, they have," the Amazon replied simply. "Best way is for us to go and see—and we will. Now, enough of your dreaming, Abna. Get a space suit on and be ready to make the jump into the emergency machine when I draw the *Ultra* level."

ABOUT THE AUTHOR

British writer **JOHN RUSSELL FEARN** was born near Manchester, England, in 1908. As a child he devoured the science fiction of Wells and Verne, and was a voracious reader of the Boys' Story Papers. He was also fascinated by the cinema, and first broke into print in 1931 with a series of articles in *Film Weekly*.

He then quickly sold his first novel, *The Intelligence Gigantic*, to the American magazine, *Amazing Stories*. Over the next fifteen years, writing under several pseudonyms, Fearn became one of the most prolific contributors to all of the leading US science fiction pulps, including such legendary publications as *Astounding Stories*, *Startling Stories*, *Thrilling Wonder Stories*, and *Weird Tales*.

During the late 1940s he diversified into writing novels for the UK market, and also created his famous superwoman character, The Golden Amazon, for the prestigious Canadian magazine, the Toronto *Star Weekly*. In the early 1950s in the UK, his fifty-two novels as "Vargo Statten" were bestsellers, most notably his novelization of the film, *Creature from the Black Lagoon*.

Apart from science fiction, he had equal success with westerns, romances, and detective fiction, writing an amazing total of 180 novels—most of them in a period of just ten years—before his early death in 1960. His work has been translated into nine languages, and continues to be reprinted and read worldwide.

www.ingramcontent.com/pod-product-compliance
Lightning Source LLC
Chambersburg PA
CBHW022151260626
47155CB00017B/1835